A BROOKHAVEN PARANORMAL COZY MYSTERY
BOOK 9

# HIGH ROLLER

## S.E. BIGLOW

If you enjoy this work, please consider leaving a review.

For information contact; www.sarah-biglow.com

Edited by Alecia Goodman, Under Wraps Publishing

Cover Design by: Deranged Doctor Design

ISBN: 978-1-955988-73-5

Published by S.E. Biglow: February 2026

10 9 8 7 6 5 4 3 2 1

# SPECIAL THANKS

I would like to thank all of the wonderful backers who supported this series on Kickstarter and made these books possible.

I need to give an extra special shout out to Heiko Koenig, GhostCat, pjs, John Idler, Sandy K., Anonymous Reader, Monica Kim, Matthew Walker, Ayl, Elizabeth W., Stephen Ballentine, Tracy 'Rayon' Fretwell, Julie McAtee, Melissa Showers, Kim, Kathy, Will 'It Work' Dansicker, Lisa Spaulding, Karin Baxter, Melissa, M. Kramer, Alexandra Corrsin, Katie, maileguy, Louisa Kannberg, Rob Steinberger, Brian, Anna McCluskey, Vannessa, Bridgette M. Findley, Mary E. Tallini, Amy Gentilini, Rosa, Stephanie Thomas, Taylor Park, Toby Rodgers, David Blethen, Amelia Pluck and Bonniejean Boettcher,

**1**

The energy at the B&B as I walked down the stairs to the first floor was charged. I moved through the familiar space with a tangible sense of anticipation I couldn't quite pinpoint. Nothing had changed recently. The town had resumed it's normal level of intrigue—that was to say none—since the summer's carnival murder.

"You look contemplative," Tania noted when I walked into the kitchen. She stood in front of the stove flipping perfectly round pancakes.

"Just thinking," I muttered and poured myself a cup of coffee. "We aren't expecting any new boarders, are we?"

"Not until next week. Why do you ask?" Tania remained focused on preparing breakfast.

"It could be nothing, but I'm getting this weird feeling."

My landlady set down her spatula and turned to face me. "Feelings are typically my department. Maybe I can help?"

Well, she wasn't wrong. As the resident empath, she was much more in tune with sensing and interpreting emotions than the rest of us. She made a 'go on' gesture at me.

"It's like the air in the B&B is charged ... the whole building senses that something's coming. I know it sounds mental. I just can't shake the feeling that the universe is trying to tell me something is on its way."

"Oh, that is interesting," she said with a noncommittal shoulder shrug. "Do you have anything you expect to happen soon? At work perhaps?"

I shook my head and took another sip of coffee. "Not that I can think of. I mean I have some new seedlings I've been nurturing, and they've been doing really well. But nothing out of the ordinary."

"Well, anything going on with Maggie?"

"We're having dinner later, just a normal date. Not anything important I can think of." After all, our anniversary wasn't until February. And while the ride we'd taken on the Ferris wheel when Silvan's murder had been solved was quite romantic, there hadn't been any major forward movement in our relationship. Sure, I spent most weekends at her flat and some weeknights, too. But we hadn't taken any steps to move in together. The B&B was still very much my home.

"Then maybe something's coming and you just have to be patient until you find out what it is," Tania stated and pivoted to transfer the pancakes to a serving plate. "It has been a while since you've had something to puzzle out. Maybe the universe is giving you a new mystery to solve."

I disliked feeling like I was missing a clue. Though Tania could be right. Maybe the universe was just giving me a heads up that something was on the horizon. Not that I wanted any harm to befall anyone in town. But I couldn't deny the rush I got from putting all the pieces together on a case. Ginny Hayes had somewhat affectionately dubbed me an amateur detective and the longer I lived in Brookhaven, the more I didn't mind the moniker.

"Sit, have something to eat," Tania suggested, setting the serving plate on the table beside the butter and maple syrup.

"You know it's really unfair," Sam bemoaned, materializing beside the table. He sported a red sequined jacket and tight leather pants, the color of rust.

"What's not fair?" I addressed the ghost, sitting down and piling three of the pancakes onto a plate. Tania set out some strawberry jam, too, and some freshly sliced bananas.

"That I have to watch you eat food that smells amazing."

"Well, I appreciate that you enjoy my cooking," Tania admitted and sat down to join me.

I eyed the ghost with skepticism. He'd never complained about being unable to indulge in things like eating and drinking. Not even when Ginny and Rick's ancestors had temporarily possessed living hosts. "What's got you in a mood?"

He blinked at me, as if confused by my question. He shot Tania a sideways glance before he crossed his arms over his chest and gave me an exaggerated eye roll. "Can't a guy just be jealous every now and again? I may not act like it, but this existence can be lonely sometimes."

"You've got loads of friends," I countered.

"I've got you, Tania, and Maggie. My social circle isn't exactly expanding."

"You've got Beau, too ... Ginny and Rick. And I suppose Vinnie when you're in the mood to let him see you."

"And they don't understand my plight."

Today was just so weird.

Ignoring the ghost as he continued to bemoan his lack of friends, I tucked into my food, trying my best not to let his continued presence bother me. Eventually, he flounced out of my field of vision. Why did he suddenly care so much about having friends? Though I could see his point. Why, of all days, did he bring it up today?

"So, where are you and Maggie going for dinner?" Tania sipped her mug and gave me an intense expression.

"Maggie said it's a surprise."

"Hmm ... A day full of unknowns then."

I smiled, nodding as I finished my breakfast. My phone beeped, reminding me to leave the house now, so I wouldn't be late for work. Tania offered me a wave as I hurried out of the kitchen, through the foyer, and onto the front porch. I spotted Beau lounging on the railing, barely indistinguishable from the wood's grain.

"See you later, mate," I called.

Beau didn't offer any response as I left the B&B

behind. Trying to shake the unease from my mind, I focused on the familiar walk down Main Street. I spotted a car parked in front of High Time as I arrived. That was odd since we weren't open to the public yet. Most of the kitchen staff weren't even on shift at this time. I walked around to the back and entered through the employee door, passing through the kitchen and break room. I stowed my bag in a locker and with my key unlocked the door to the grow room.

I could hear muffled voices coming from the front of the shop. I crept closer to the door that led to the front counter and register, pressing my ear to the crack between its surface and the frame.

"You're sure no one's told her?" Sage's voice carried.

"Would I lie to you?" Ginny replied.

I resisted the urge to fling the door open and interrupt their conversation. Still, without realizing I'd done it, one of the plants lining the wall to my left extended a leaf outward, squeezing through the tiny space. I could feel the plant's desire, urging me to take hold and use my magic for a little light snooping.

I lightly pinched the stem and my vision went green. The front room filled my vision, and I could see Ginny standing on the far side of the counter, holding a clipboard. Sage faced her next to the register.

"You've confirmed everything?" Sage continued.

Ginny held up the clipboard. "All accounted for. Have you figured out what you're bringing yet?"

Sage shook her head, the very tips of her aqua do fluttering. "I mean what do you get someone for something like this? It's not exactly normal."

Ginny set the clipboard down and leaned in. "I asked Rick what he was getting, and my brother looked at me like a deer caught in headlights."

"I had thought everyone got the memo about the requirements."

"Apparently not. My brother claimed he was busy," she explained and used her hands to make air quotes, "but he's never been into this sort of thing. Trust me, holidays in our house growing up were ... uh, interesting because of his aversion to being prepared."

Just then, Ginny turned, and her eyes widened. She pressed her finger to her lips, gestured at the very tip of the leaf poking out from behind the door. Sage followed where she pointed and mouthed something that could have been, 'Really?' Ginny simply nodded and Sage moved around the counter to join the her. Together they hurried outside, leaving me alone.

I pulled my hand away from the plant and its stem and leaves receded to their normal position. Whatever the women had been planning, they didn't want me to know about it. But why? A moment later, I picked out the sounds of the bell jingling over the front door. I busied myself with tending the plants in the farthest bay from the door separating the front from the grow room.

The door opened and Sage appeared. "Morning, Darcy. I didn't see you come in." She gave no hint that she knew I'd been eavesdropping.

"Just getting things going for the day," I replied, trying to act as if I hadn't overheard her and Ginny's conversation.

"Good." After a moment she added, "Have I told you how grateful I am to have you as an employee?"

"Uh, I mean not recently. But I know you appreciate my particular skillset. I owe you so much, too. If it weren't for you, I wouldn't have the opportunity to be here, to grow as a witch, and to find where I belonged."

"I guess it was fate we crossed paths then," she said with a beaming smile. "I'll see you later."

I offered her a one-handed wave, my other hand

preoccupied with coaxing a seedling that had gone droopy overnight. That sense of anticipation I'd picked up on at the B&B returned. Wiping my hands on my jeans, I retrieved my phone and texted Maggie.

> You sure you can't tell me anything about where we're going tonight? Curiosity has my head spinning.

I waited for what seemed ages for her to reply. A tiny bubble and three dots appeared, disappeared, and reappeared again. Finally, my girlfriend replied.

> I told you it's a surprise. I'll pick you up after work.

I glanced down at my outfit.

> Why not the B&B? I want to change before we go.

Her response came quicker this time.

> What you've got on is perfect.

The fact she didn't want me to change out of my work clothes was suspect. Surely, if Maggie were taking me to a nice dinner, she wouldn't want me covered in bits of plant debris and dirt. But I wasn't about to argue with her. I'd just have to wait and see where we ended up tonight.

I MANAGED to distract myself through lunch and the early afternoon hours. As I headed for the break room to clock out, I noticed some of the other employees casting furtive glances my way, including Thomas. He'd changed out of his uniform and was disentangling his dreads from the hairnet around his head.

"Have I done something to offend you?" I asked him bluntly.

His fingers stopped moving as the end of the net snagged on the dread in his hand. "What?"

"You all keep looking at me like I've done something wrong. And when I stopped by Ginny's at lunch today, she purposely disappeared. I feel like I must have committed some sort of offense, because everyone's been acting strange around me all day."

Thomas managed to free his hair and tossed the disposable hairnet in a nearby trash can. "You didn't do anything Darcy. I swear. Just ... not many of us last very long in a job like this. And well, it's been a while, you know?"

I stared at him. "Oh, right."

"All I'm saying is we're glad you're around. You make things interesting."

I wasn't so sure about that. I might fancy myself to be an amateur detective, but strange happenings seemed to follow me. Or at least they liked to unfold in close proximity to me.

My phone buzzed with an incoming message from Maggie letting me know she was outside. "Well, uh, I'm glad to be here, too. I need to get going though. Dinner with Maggie."

"Have fun."

I hurried out the employee door and rounded the side of the building to find Maggie parked in almost the same spot the car—which I now realized had to belong to Ginny—had sat. I couldn't make out much of my girlfriend's attire through the passenger side window, but she didn't appear to be dressed much different than usual.

I climbed in and gave her a kiss before putting on my seatbelt. "Do I get to know where we're going now?"

She shook her head and held out a length of cloth. "Put this on."

"You can't be serious."

"Just trust me."

"I do. But I don't like not knowing where I'm going."

"You are going to love it. I promise."

Sucking in a deep breath, I tied the blindfold over my eyes. I'd hoped the fabric might be thin enough to see outlines through it, but no such luck. Instead, I tried to use my other senses to pinpoint where we might be heading. I could make out the faint chatter of pedestrian conversations on the sidewalks, but they quickly vanished. The car sped up, stopped, and made a series of turns. Without being able to see, my stomach sloshed, and I began taking slow, deep breaths to keep my body in check.

Maggie must have noticed the change in my breathing. Although she continued making periodic turns, they weren't nearly as sharp or aggressive. I gripped the door handle as I braced for another turn. Only it didn't come.

"Almost there?" I managed to get out the words in between steadying breaths.

"Almost."

The car slowed down and rolled to a stop before making a slow, bumpy turn. The terrain beneath us changed to something more spongy. We'd gone off road. Finally, the engine cut out and I heard Maggie unclip her seatbelt. Fumbling blindly, I did the same. In the time it took to disentangle myself from the belt, Maggie had exited the driver side and came around to open my door.

"Give me your hands."

She took each of my hands in hers and pulled me to my feet.

I felt grass beneath my shoes as we moved forward, a few steps at a time. Maggie continued ahead of me, giving my hands a squeeze now and again to signal I was doing well.

"We have to be almost there," I protested.

Maggie released my left hand. I heard something swing ahead of me, perhaps a gate.

My right hand warmed beneath Maggie's touch and the pangs of anxiety that I'd felt bubbling up, receded. Despite being on the lawn, my magic refused to give me a helping hand. Maybe the universe didn't want to ruin the surprise either?

We passed where I'd heard the gate and finally stopped walking. Maggie let go of my other hand and bumped my right shoulder, letting me know she'd moved to stand beside me. That same sense of anticipation washed over me again, more intense than it had been earlier.

"Can I take this bloody thing off now?"

"Yeah. You can remove the blindfold." Maggie's voice was giddy.

I tugged the fabric over my head and blinked as the afternoon sunlight momentarily blinded me. When my vision resolved, I found myself in Tania's backyard looking at all of my friends gathered together.

"Surprise!"

2

It took me a minute to register the full extent of the group assembled in the B&B's garden. A handful of my High Time colleagues, including Thomas, stood in the back. Ginny, Sage, and Tania were up front and center. Even Chief Hayes and Vinnie had joined in. But what were they surprising me for?

"Not that I am opposed to surprises, but ... I've clearly missed something because it's not my birthday," I managed.

Maggie pivoted to stand in front of me, fixing me with a wide grin. "Do you really not remember?"

I shook my head, confused.

"Darcy, you've been living here in Brookhaven for two years!" Maggie's eyes sparkled with excitement.

The pieces slowly clicked into place. How had I been so oblivious to the milestone? A year ago, I'd been acutely aware of this anniversary. Lately, so much was happening in my life, I suppose I'd lost track. It was touching to see that the people I'd come to consider family hadn't failed to mark the occasion. I peered over at Ginny and Sage, offering them a sheepish laugh.

"I guess now I know why you were talking about presents this morning."

Ginny swatted at Sage's arm. "I knew she was spying on us."

I turned my attention to the far side of the yard, where a set of folding tables had been erected. One held trays of food, artfully laid out, while the other contained a few small gift boxes and colorful bags.

"You're not very good at being the center of attention," Sam chided, appearing beside me as Maggie let go of my hands.

"I take it this is what had you in a tiff this morning?" I made a sweeping gesture towards the food.

"Well, it does seem awfully unfair that everyone gets to enjoy it all, and I'm left on the sidelines watching." His faux annoyance disappeared, and his expression turned serious. "Darcy, I am really glad you've stuck around. My afterlife would be exceeding boring without you."

"I'm glad I stuck around, too." I jutted my chin towards the gifts. "Is it an American thing to give gifts at these sorts of gatherings?"

Sam shrugged one sequined shoulder. "I think you're probably just extra special."

I wasn't going to refuse being appreciated, especially by the people I'd come to call family in Brookhaven. As discreetly as possible, I made my way toward the tables and poked at the first gift, a bright purple paper bag with a deep green ribbon securing the handles together.

"I hope you like it." Vinnie's voice came from behind me, and I barely avoided jumping in surprise.

"You all really didn't have to do any of this," I protested. "I mean, I'm grateful for the relationships I've cultivated with everyone ... and for them to take the time out of their day to celebrate my anniversary here. But I'm just one person."

"You've made a difference in the lives of every person here, Darcy. Even if it wasn't magically. You're a good friend. You care about the people in your orbit, and you fight for them fiercely. It doesn't go unnoticed."

I felt heat warm the nape of my neck at his words. Sam was right. I was rubbish at being in the spotlight. "Vinnie, dare I ask what's inside?" I picked up the package and made a show of examining it.

"I don't think anyone is going to stop you from opening it whenever you want. It's your party, as they say."

Vinnie watched me intently as I set the bag down again and carefully untied the bow. The ribbon fell to the table, and I reached inside, pulling out a small box. My heart skipped a beat as I studied it, if I wasn't mistaken, it looked almost like a jewelry box. I cast Vinnie another look and he made a 'go on' gesture. My fingers grew sweaty as I fumbled to open the box.

A small pendant in the shape of a deputy badge sat nestled inside on a delicate silver chain. I could make out the words, 'Honorary Deputy' etched into the design. I grinned at Vinnie. "This is really sweet."

"It's from Rick and me both. Tyson helped pick it out, too. We aren't exactly jewelry connoisseurs."

"I love it." I couldn't help but laugh as I set it aside. For months now, Vinnie had been telling me he ought to just deputize me, given how many times I had helped the department solve cases. This pendant was as close as he was going to get.

"I am honestly surprised we managed to keep this from you," Rick admitted, stepping up on Vinnie's left.

"Well, apparently I'm quite easily lied to," I replied and held up the pendant. "I hear this is from you. Thanks, Chief."

"Gifts aren't really my forte."

That tracked with Ginny's earlier comment. Speaking of his sister, she was busy filling a plate with food before making a beeline for me. She held it out to me.

"The guest of honor can't go hungry."

Not that I'd ever turn down Tania's cooking, but my appetite seemed to flee under the scrutiny of everyone around. Seeing me awkwardly holding the gift from Rick and Vinnie, Ginny set the plate down and plucked the delicate chain from my fingers. Without asking permission, she spun me around and secured it at the nape of my neck.

"Two years ago, I wouldn't have even considered this sort of gathering, especially celebrating someone who didn't grow up here. But Darcy, you've helped me realize that not all new things or people are dangerous or unwanted," she said when I turned back to face her. "Now, come sit and eat. Host's orders."

Tania spotted me watching her and gave a small wave. She indicated one of the chairs that had been moved from their usual place right outside the back door. Ginny pressed the plate of food into my hands again and I made my way across the yard to sit. Along the way, I gave the other guests, including Thomas, a nod of acknowledgement.

"You know, I expected you to be more overwhelmed than you are," Tania said softly when I sat down.

"Oh, I am plenty overwhelmed. I guess this explains the strange feeling I've had all day. Even before I overheard Sage and Ginny talking at High Time this morning."

"I will admit, I did not like deceiving you ... but Maggie and Ginny insisted on this celebration and making it a surprise."

"I know everyone's thanking me for what I've done in Brookhaven the last two years, but I owe you as much thanks. If it weren't for you, none of this would have been possible."

She waved off my gratitude. "Don't be silly."

"If I hadn't come to stay at your B&B, if you hadn't been so welcoming and supportive of the magic I was terrified to use, I never would have been comfortable uprooting my life and coming here for a fresh start. Without your guidance, I wouldn't be the witch I am today. If anything, we should be celebrating you, too."

"I don't mind sharing the spotlight if you insist."

"I do."

Tania stood and clapped her hands together. The space fell silent, and all eyes were on my landlady. "Thank you all for coming today. This is not a formal gathering, so make yourselves at home. And please get something to eat."

Taking that as their cue, my work friends descended on the table of food. I searched the crowd for Maggie, finally spotting her in conversation with Tyson, who I hadn't noticed earlier. Maggie caught me staring and offered me a smile, but didn't halt the discussion. Focusing my attention on the plate of food in my lap, I busied myself with enjoying the meal Tania had prepared. It was a delicious mix of rice, plantains, and pulled pork along with some salad and thick slices of home-made bread. Party goers passed by my seat, offering me their congratulations as they waited in line for food.

Scanning the crowd, a pang of sadness washed over me. This would have been something I'd love to share with my cousin Piper or Nan. Except Piper was busy traveling and Nan wasn't about to make the trip across the pond for a small celebration.

*'Conflicting emotions.'*

Beau's voice echoed in my head as I set my now-empty plate on the grass by my feet. I looked down as the chameleon settled across my legs, making no attempt to hide himself from the guests around us. Even when it was just Tania, Sam, and I at the B&B, he was usually more comfortable blending in with his surroundings. Besides, he could communicate without the need to be seen.

"Yeah, a bit," I replied. "But mostly happy emotions. It's just wishful thinking about having my family here, too."

*'Chosen family is good.'*

"Yeah, I know, mate. Believe me, I would choose all of you any day. But still, some things you just wish you could experience with the people who share your DNA."

The reptile gave a small head bob, as if to nod his understanding. I reached out and stroked the tip of my right index finger along the scales on his back. "I already said how grateful I am to Tania for how she changed my life. And I should tell you how much you mean to me, too."

*'My chosen family, too.'*

"You definitely were the one who chose me," I agreed. "I still don't quite know why, but I'm really happy you did. You've made the past two years of my life really magical. And yeah, I realize how cheesy that sounds."

"I'd say it's more corny than cheesy," Ginny interjected, sitting down in the chair beside me. "You know, you have more gifts to open."

"I think I'll save them for later and open on my own, if people don't mind. I think that whole being overwhelmed thing is starting to hit me after all."

"Yeah, I don't think anyone's going to argue with you about that."

"I still can't believe you and Maggie put all of this together."

"Like I said, you matter to the people around here. Besides, we needed something good to celebrate, with all the awfulness that keeps coming to town these days."

I appreciated how Ginny didn't insinuate that I was the cause of all the unpleasantness that had befallen Brookhaven since my arrival. There was a time when she would have placed the blame squarely on my shoulders for being the outsider.

"Well, hopefully there won't be any more bad things coming to town any time soon," I said.

Ginny snorted. "You realize now you've jinxed it."

"Oh come on, you can't really believe in that sort of thing."

"We are witches, we cast magic spells that manipulate the world around us. You bet I believe jinxes are real. Mark my words, you put that out into the universe, it's going to come back and bite you." Ginny levered herself out of the chair and stepped into the line for food again.

Her words didn't exactly bolster my mood. Maggie finally pulled herself away from her conversation with Tyson and moved in my direction. After reaching Beau and I, she bent down to give the reptile a pet on the head and planted a kiss on my lips. "I hope you aren't too disappointed that we aren't having some fancy, intimate dinner."

"You know I'd never say no to anything Tania cooked. And I really do appreciate everyone's support." I was beginning to feel like a broken record.

"I'll make it up to you, promise," she vowed, sitting beside me. "I just wanted you to know how special you are to everyone here, me included."

"I know how special I am to you. You remind me every day by loving me," I told her.

"Still, I feel like I owe you a nice dinner out somewhere, all dressed up, for tricking you."

"Well, I won't say no to a date night," I agreed.

She grinned at me, the expression crinkling the skin around her eyes as she looked at me. Even Ginny's proclamation that I had tempted fate couldn't possibly ruin the evening. People chatted around us, dipping in and out of their own conversations to say hello to me and share their own reasons for why they wanted to be here. Sage stopped beside my chair just as the sun dipped below the trees around us.

"You should already know I'm grateful for everything you do," she said. "I need to head out. I'll see you at work tomorrow."

I gave her a small salute. "See you then boss."

She laughed and pivoted on her heel, weaving between the thinning crowd . Sage disappeared through the side gate Maggie and I had entered. I eyed the table with its mostly empty serving trays and depleted flatware and utensils. I also noticed Tania was absent.

"There's going to be some big dessert, right?" Without thinking I was on my feet, Beau scurried to resettle on the arm of the chair before he tumbled from my lap.

"Maybe," Maggie replied.

I stepped over to the folding table and began gathering up and stacking the platters to make them easier to carry inside. Maggie tried to shoo me away, but I ignored her. The B&B was still my home, and I could clear away dirty dishes if I wanted. Rick saw me approaching the back door and pulled it open, not questioning my motives. He gave me a smile as he shut the door behind me.

I found Tania in the kitchen, setting some candied strawberries on the top of a three-tiered chocolate cake with dark chocolate ganache. It smelled heavenly.

"Oh, Darcy, *dame esos.*" She made a grabbing motion for the plates and serving forks I'd piled up.

"Come on. I may be the guest of honor, but that doesn't mean I can just ignore dirty dishes."

"Gracias, but your place tonight is out there, mingling with your guests and being celebrated. I will handle the dishes."

"I tried to stop her," Maggie called from behind me.

"I just want to feel useful," I protested.

"Here, you can take the dessert plates and forks out to the table. And then you can sit down and enjoy being catered to." Tania pressed small paper plates and plastic forks into my hand.

"I'm going to get started on the tea and coffee," Maggie announced and set the percolator working and filled the kettle with water to boil.

Depositing the plates and forks on the table in the garden took no time at all. I was about to resume my seat when I realized the regular beverages had run out. It seemed rude to assume guests would want a hot drink with their cake. I returned to the kitchen just in time to hear the doorbell ring.

Maggie and I reacted in unison, moving to the front foyer. She beat me to the door by a split second and pulled it open. A tall man with a mop of messy reddish-brown hair stood on the front steps.

"Hey Magpie," he greeted, looking directly at Maggie.

<br>

**3**

ime stood still on the B&B's front porch as Maggie stared at the man opposite her. The pet name he'd used was unfamiliar to me and the way her jaw tightened suggested it wasn't one she was fond of. I reached for her left hand and gave it a reassuring squeeze, if only to remind her that I was with her.

"Aren't you going to invite me in?" the man asked, giving her a lopsided grin.

Maggie's fingers trembled in mine as she tried to regain her composure. Realizing she wasn't quite ready to explain, I stepped up and offered the man my free hand. "Darcy Ingram. And you are?"

"Max Henley."

*Maggie's brother.*

Maggie finally jolted from her frozen state and pulled her hand free of mine, so she could cross her arms over her chest. "What are you doing here, Max?"

"Can't a guy come say hi to his favorite sister?"

She gave him a pointed look. "No, not when I'm your only sister and it's been years. This isn't even my house. How'd you find me here?"

"Come on, Magpie, don't be like that."

Clearing my throat, I pulled Maggie back from the front door. I turned to Max, and said, "Just give us a minute."

I shut the door and pulled my girlfriend onto the landing at the bottom of the stairs. "Maggie, talk to me."

Her gaze flitted to the door and back to me. "I told you about my brother and his gambling problems. He only ever shows up if he wants something. Usually money. The last time he came asking, I told him I didn't want to see him again."

"I mean, that's harsh, but if you were trying to help him address an addiction, it makes sense. Maybe things have turned around?"

"I would love to think things have changed. But Darcy I know my brother, and as much as I love him, I believe he's incapable of change."

I knew something was left unsaid. I could see the pain in her eyes, something more than simply feeling hurt and used by an addict chasing his next gambling high. "There's more to the story, isn't there?"

She squirmed under my gaze. "I'm a healer, Darcy. I'm meant to make people better. But everything I tried failed to fix him. Nothing helped."

"You can't save everyone, Maggie. You've got to know that."

Tears sparkled in her blue irises, but she refused to let them fall. "I guess family is complicated."

"Believe me. I'm the queen of complicated families, remember?"

"At least I'm not alone in the crazy family department," she admitted with a small hiccup of laughter. She wiped at the unshed tears. Clear-eyed, she opened the door again. Max still stood there, looking hopeful.

"You are really here to visit?"

He gave a nod. "I just wanted to see my sister."

"Darcy, who's at the door?" Tania called from the kitchen.

"Guess you better come in, then," Maggie said and opened the door wide enough for Max to enter.

He stepped into the foyer and looked around the

space. Our gazes met briefly, and I could feel him assessing me. Could he sense my relationship with Maggie? In the back of my mind, I wondered what sort of magic her brother possessed. If it was anything like Vinnie's uncle, I could understand the difficulty he had with quitting gambling. Still, we'd just met. It wasn't my place to interrogate him.

"Tania, this is my brother, Max," Maggie introduced, leading him into the kitchen where Tania stood putting the finishing touches on the cake.

"Welcome. You're visiting at a wonderful time," she exclaimed, wiping her hands on her apron before offering him a quick hug and kiss on the cheek.

"Someone's birthday?" He eyed the cake.

"More like an anniversary celebration. It's my anniversary of living in Brookhaven," I blurted in one long breath, suddenly feeling self-conscious about the festivities.

"Guess I did come at a good time then."

"Did we lose the guest of honor?" Ginny called from the back door. "People think you've pulled a disappearing act."

"We have a surprise visitor." I gestured to Max. "But the more the merrier, right?"

Ginny gave him an appraising look before saying, "It's your party."

Max rubbed his hands together before pointing at the cake. "I can take that out if you want."

"Thank you." Tania untied the apron from around her waist, slid it over her head, and hung it on the front of the oven.

I watched him navigate the door leading to the back yard and felt Tania's hand on my shoulder. "Don't tell Maggie, but I think he's not being entirely truthful."

"What do you mean?"

"He may look okay, but the anxiety wafting off him is as heavy as cheap cologne. Something is weighing on his heart and his mind. I fear he needs to let it out."

Maggie had said that Max only ever dropped by when he needed money. Maybe that was all it was now. Not the best reason for him to drop by, but an understandable one. And maybe he assumed enough time had passed that Maggie wouldn't turn him away outright, especially in front of a group of people.

However, that did raise the question of him knowing where to find her. He'd evaded her question about it. I rejoined the festivities in the yard to find Max artfully slicing up the cake and plating it. If I didn't know any better, I'd guess he had experience in food service. He offered me a piece with a dramatic hand flourish.

"Thanks." I stood holding the cake as he watched me. "You and my sister, you're together?"

"As a matter of fact, yes we are. Is that a problem?"

"No. I'm glad she found someone that makes her happy. At least I'm assuming you make her happy."

"I like to think so." I took a bite of cake, savoring the sweetness and lightness of the confection. "But can I ask you something?" He shrugged and I took it as tacit permission to continue. "How did you know to find Maggie here?"

"You sound just like her, wanting to know everything about what I'm doing."

"I think it's a fair question. This isn't her house. She doesn't even stay here overnight. And as far as I know she didn't post about this event anywhere. Everyone wanted to keep it a surprise from me. So, I think you owe her an explanation at the very least."

"It's not that big of a deal," he said.

I gestured where Rick stood between Ginny and Sage. "That man is the Chief of Police. He also happens to have some very unique supernatural abilities. I don't think you want to get on his bad side. And he is rather fond of your sister. So, how did you find her here?"

"I may have hacked her private messages online, okay? It's been a while and I knew she wouldn't answer my calls or texts, so I kind of snooped. Don't tell the cop. Please."

The way his voice cracked, shifting from smug to pleading caught my attention. The pressure he applied on my right arm as he spoke, grabbing me to make his point, wasn't lost on me either. Tania was right. This man was concealing some serious anxiety. I didn't need to be an empath to pick up on it.

"You two really were like peas in a pod when younger, weren't you?" I replied. "Maggie's been known to do a little extra curricular online snooping from time to time."

"Where do you think I learned it all from?"

It confirmed that Maggie had been coordinating today's events with others—likely Ginny—via private message. At least that solved one small mystery.

"You came here for some other reason, not just to see Maggie. She told me she'd basically cut you off the last time you came around asking for anything."

"Uh, things have changed. I've changed."

I wasn't the one he needed to tell. Maggie had distanced herself from her brother, sticking to the fringes of the gathered group off by the side gate. Still, I sensed Max wasn't entirely honest with me. I was a stranger to him. He had no reason to entrust me with anything private. Clearly, he was either scared or too ashamed of whatever it was to come clean to Maggie on his own. So, that meant getting a little help from our resident human lie detector. Maggie was my person after all, and I needed to protect her.

"Will you excuse me? I need to help Tania with the tea and coffee," I said, pivoting on my heel and heading back into the kitchen. Tania had already taken the coffee out, walking around offering it to the guests one by one. I noticed the kettle was missing from the stove. She must have brought that out, too. Well, I hadn't really intended to help my landlady. I pulled out my phone and dialed Ginny's number.

I watched from the kitchen window as Ginny stopped talking mid-conversation with Rick and answered her phone. "Darcy, did you pocket dial me?"

"I need you to come to the kitchen."

She glanced my way before hanging up and walking inside. "You could have just texted."

"I figured a call was harder to ignore." I pointed to Max as he continued to serve cake. "Have you ever met Maggie's brother before?"

"Nope. But I would have pegged him as related to her a mile off."

"Tania says he's wafting anxiety, and I get the sense he's keeping something close to the vest. He claimed he just wanted to pay his sister a visit. But she told me the last time they spoke, she told him she wasn't willing to see him anymore."

"And you want me to get him to open up."

"Please if there's something going on and it affects Maggie, it affects all of us."

"You don't have to twist my arm. She's my friend, too. But if it's three against one, that could spook him."

"You have another suggestion?"

"Get Maggie to try and introduce him around. Most of the people out there don't know who he is. I can strike up a conversation with him and see what I get out of him."

It was worth a shot. Maggie deserved to know the real reason her brother had come to town. Ginny left the kitchen first, returning to Rick and Sage. I was about to leave when I sensed a presence behind me. I made a quarter turn to find Sam hovering in the middle of the kitchen.

"You holding up okay with all the guests?"

"I am perfectly capable of existing around a bunch of living people eating and drinking and making merry. But you've got that look you get when things are about to get ... weird."

"I have no idea what you're talking about."

"You know that little twinkle in your eye when you find a mystery to unravel. A question that you just have to answer. Maggie's hunky brother is a big, bold question mark that you can't help but turn into a period."

"I think you're off your rocker, mate. I just want him to be truthful with Maggie about why he's here. That's all. I'm supporting my girlfriend."

"Say what you will, but mark my words. This one's going to turn into some crazy treasure hunt before you know it."

I waved off his warning and wound my way through the thinning crowd to stand beside Maggie. I got her attention, and we stepped off to one side. "I think your brother's not being entirely truthful about why he's come. Ginny's going to help, but she doesn't want it to come off like an interrogation. So, you should walk him around, introduce him to people. That way it seems less obvious when she starts asking questions."

"I'd still like to know how he found me here."

At least I could sate that curiosity. "Seems hacking is a family trait. He read your messages."

"I'm going to kill him."

"Relax. He claims to have changed."

"And yet he's hiding things," she muttered.

She exhaled slowly and I could see the tension ease from her shoulders. She strode over to Max, wrapped her arm around his shoulders, and hauled him away from the food table. She made the rounds, briefly introducing him to everyone in range. Tania came past me carrying an empty carafe of coffee.

"Things are about to get complicated." There was no hint of a question in her tone.

It was probably better that Ginny did her interrogating without an audience. Except I didn't know how to get everyone else to leave without looking ungrateful or rude.

"Hey, Darcy!" Thomas called as he crossed the lawn. "A bunch of us have to head out, but we'll see you tomorrow at work."

I offered each of my co-workers quick hugs.

"Thanks for coming. I'm glad I've made a positive impact on your lives."

Thomas smirked. "Some of them just came for the free food and cake."

I laughed. "The food was delicious; I don't blame them."

He waved and led the small contingent of High Time employees out the side gate. It made things simpler. Maggie flagged me down as she approached Rick and Ginny. Sage had wandered off to begin picking up paper plates strewn in the grass.

"And this is Ginny. She owns the cafe on Main Street," Maggie said, shoving her brother towards the pretty blonde.

Rick took a deliberate step away from the conversation. Ginny must have warned him off ahead of time. Max extended his hand to Ginny, and she took it without hesitation. "So, you're Maggie's brother. Not going to lie, she doesn't talk about you much."

Max gave a nervous laugh. "Yeah, I'm not surprised. She's the sibling who made something of her life. I'm just the one who can't shake a bad habit."

"We all have things we struggle with," Ginny replied as I moved to stand beside Maggie. I took her hand again. "You may not have the best relationship with your sister, but you came here for a reason." I could almost see a flash in Ginny's' eyes as she didn't break eye contact with him. Her hand remained firmly grasped around his, too. There was no getting away from her now.

Max's jaw worked as if he were trying to hold back his words. They came tumbling out of him, anyway, compelled by Ginny's magic. "I'm in trouble. My family's been taken, and I need help. Maggie's always been there for me, even when it was tough love. I need her help to get them back."

**4**

Max's words rang in my ears as he stood there, his hands still clenched in Ginny's grasp. The look of surprise on her face mirrored how I felt at his declaration. Maggie's face shifted from disbelief to anger to worry.

"What do you mean something's happened? I talked to Mom and Dad two days ago. They seemed fine," Maggie pressed her brother.

"Why don't we take this inside, somewhere more private?" Ginny suggested, nodding towards the B&B. She let go of Max's hands and gently ushered him towards the back door.

Rick and Vinnie stood off to one side in conversation, clearly unaware of what was happening.

Until we knew more than Max's cryptic magic-induced plea for help, that was for the best. Wordlessly, Max traipsed back into the kitchen with Maggie on his heels. Ginny followed them and I brought up the rear.

Once we'd gathered chairs around the kitchen table, Max let out a slow exhale. "It's not Mom or Dad." His hands shook as he pulled out his phone. He tapped a few times on the screen and slid it over to Maggie. "That's Chloe and our little girl, Aneesa. She's only four months old."

Maggie stared at the young woman and baby in the picture. "I didn't know you became a dad."

"I didn't really tell a lot of people. Most of the people I would have told aren't exactly the best influences."

"Wait. Do Mom and Dad know?"

"Yeah, they came up right after Aneesa was born. And believe me, I thought I'd never hear the end of it, mom insisting I share the news with you. But I figured you didn't need to add worrying about them to your list of Max drama."

"I don't have a list of Max drama," Maggie countered. "But it would have been nice to know I had a niece."

"And a sister-in-law. We just got married at the courthouse a couple of weeks ago."

"Congratulations!" I offered. "But you mentioned they're in trouble?"

Max rubbed at his chin. "About five months ago, right before Aneesa was born, I started to get clean. Going to Gambler's Anonymous meetings and quitting cold turkey. I wanted to do right by my little girl. I didn't want her to grow up with the fear that dad was going to lose her home, you know?"

"You've been clean for five months?" Maggie sounded equal parts hopeful and shocked.

"Yeah." Tears trickled down his cheeks. "It's the hardest thing I've ever done, Maggie. But I knew it was the right thing to do. I know I needed help to stop. But I ... uh, didn't exactly leave things in a great place with Tony."

"Who's Tony?" Ginny leaned in, ready to force the truth from Max's lips if necessary.

"My bookie."

"You stopped gambling without repaying him?" Maggie leaned back in her chair, waiting for her brother to tell her she'd guessed wrong.

"I was paying him back. But things got away from me. Baby stuff is expensive, and I figured it was more important that Aneesa have formula and diapers and stuff. You know, be a real dad. So, I skipped some payments to Tony."

"Is Tony the sort of guy to get ... aggressive when you don't pay up?" I wasn't sure how else to phrase the question.

"I didn't think so. He'd always been pretty chill. It's why I liked him. But a couple weeks ago, he kept blowing up my phone, telling me I needed to pay him in full and if I didn't, he was going to make sure I had proper motivation to do it."

"And I'm guessing you didn't pay him." My heart hammered double time against my ribs.

"I tried, but I still owed him ten thousand dollars. I don't have that kind of money. And I swore when I got clean that I wasn't going to ask anyone else for money. No more being in debt to more than one person. I told him I could get him five hundred and begged him to let that be a good faith payment. But he told me that wasn't good enough."

"What happened to Chloe and Aneesa?" Maggie's voice was almost robotic, as if she were trying deliberately to shut off any emotion. Was she trying to protect herself from the worst-case scenario?

The tears flowed free now as Max explained, "I came home from work yesterday and found the place trashed. Plates smashed in the kitchen, clothes all over the place like someone had broken in and just gotten really pissed off."

"And they were gone?" Maggie's cheeks had gone deathly pale.

"I found a note on the kitchen table. It said if I wanted to see them again, I needed to get the money I owed Tony and pay up in the next three days."

"Did you get proof they were okay?" The words barely came out of my mouth at an audible level.

"I called Tony as soon as I found the note and I demanded to know what he'd done with them. He told me to shove it and hung up. But twenty minutes later I got this photo." He closed out of the personal photo of his wife and baby girl, and brought up a text message from Tony. It showed a very scared looking Chloe clutching baby Aneesa to her chest. The baby looked to be mid-wail in her mother's embrace.

"What made you come here?" Ginny sounded almost like she was channeling her brother.

"I may not talk to Maggie much anymore, but our mom and dad love talking about everything she's doing. How you're dating someone really amazing and that you've gotten into a few scrapes in the last few months. But the two of you seem to have a knack for getting out of them and putting the bad guys behind bars."

"I'm not a cop, Max."

"Speaking of cops, maybe we ought to bring Rick and Vinnie in on this? I mean, if Max has a ransom note and we know who's got them ... surely, they could coordinate with local authorities?"

"You did report them missing, right?" Maggie's voice had gone hoarse now.

"They said I couldn't file anything yet. They haven't been gone long enough. And they think maybe I scared her and she's just hiding out some-where cooling off."

"What about the text from Tony?" I pointed to the photo on the phone screen. "Clearly, that's proof something's going on."

"They dismissed it saying that Chloe knows Tony and if he sent the picture then maybe he's helping her out."

"Does she actually know Tony?" Ginny sounded skeptical.

"They went to high school together. He tried to date her back then, but she wasn't interested. She wouldn't go anywhere with him willingly. She knows the pressure he's been putting on me."

"She knew about the debt?"

"I've always been honest with Chloe, she knew that I had a problem. But she accepted me for who I am, flaws and all. I may not have told her exactly how much I owed at first, but she knew everything after I got that text from Tony telling me to pay up."

"How exactly do you think we can help?" I pressed my forearms into the kitchen table to try and ground myself. I could feel my own emotions starting to rise to the surface. I didn't know Max or his family. But they were important to Maggie—even if she didn't like to acknowledge it most of the time —and that meant they were important to me. And the fact someone would kidnap an innocent woman and baby just to collect on a gambling debt made me angry.

"Maggie was always the better poker player. She knew all the strategies and how to deploy them."

"He means I was better at winning," Maggie stated bluntly.

"So, what are you asking for?" I glanced between brother and sister. The way Maggie's clenched fists signaled she understood his request, but wasn't happy about it.

"He wants me to play and win."

"But you can't," I said.

"Can't and shouldn't aren't the same thing," she

noted. "I shouldn't play, but that doesn't mean I can't. Max took over my old online gambling handle when I quit. I'm assuming it's still active."

"I mean, as of five months ago, yeah. There's a big tournament this weekend, five hundred dollar buy-in with big stakes. I'm sure if you just played a few hands, and got a few rounds in, you could win the rest of what I owe Tony. Then I can pay him off and get my family back."

"Let us talk to Rick and Vinnie. I'm sure they can put pressure on the police in your town and explain the situation. Rick can be very persuasive," I insisted.

Max shook his head. "It's not going to work. Just trust me, okay. I have to pay them. It's the only way to get my family back."

I detested the idea. Maggie hadn't shared the true depth of her own addiction with me; just enough to know that being around any place that involved gambling made her nervous. Even the horse track Vinnie's family owned had made her uncomfortable. I wanted to tell them both that gambling wasn't an option, but Maggie was an adult capable of making her own decisions. I needed to be a good girlfriend and support whatever she decided to do.

"What if I gave you the money?" Maggie asked, looking her brother dead in the face.

"No. I'm not going to owe you. Remember you said you weren't going to front me cash anymore, Maggie. I'm not going to make you go back on that. Your integrity matters too much to you. We both know that."

"Fine, I'll do it."

Clearly Ginny didn't approve of the plan, because she pressed her lips into a frown and stood up. Without ceremony, she grabbed Maggie by the forearm and dragged her into the dining room. I hurried after them.

"This is a really bad idea," Ginny began. "You can't put your own sobriety at risk for him."

"I have spent most of my adult life trying to help him break this addiction. If I let him try to win enough to settle his debt, he's likely to lose even more. He was never a great card player. Honestly, he wanted to impress me and gambling be something we had in common. No, if there's any chance of bringing Chloe and the baby home safely, I need to do this."

"Does anyone else find it strange that the police didn't believe him?" I blurted.

"From what my parents said, Max was a bit notorious around town as being the gambler who couldn't keep a winning streak. He's not what I'd call an alcoholic, but he could get a little rowdy when he drank. My guess is the police have seen him like that and figured he went on a losing streak. And then Chloe took off with the baby," Maggie explained.

"And think about it, if he's the one who found the place a mess with the note, and they didn't want to believe him ... Well, they could easily say he wrote the note to get back at his bookie just because he was trying to collect on a debt," Ginny added.

Maggie turned to me. "Look, I appreciate you looking out for me. I know that's why you're worried. But I have to do this for my brother. Nothing I did before worked. But I can feel it in my bones, that this will work, if I can bring his family home, this will be the healing he needs from me."

"I will support you, no matter what ... just tell me how I can help."

"I'm going to get set up for the tournament. It would be good if you two could go to his place and determine if he's actually telling the truth."

"But you said you believed him," Ginny snorted.

"And I do, but maybe we'll get lucky and find something that might tell us what actually happened." She looked at me. "You know ... like what we did at the carnival."

Assuming Max and Chloe had any living house-plants in their home, I could use my magic. I could see what had happened in the last day or two and confirm his story. "We'll go right now."

Maggie led the way back into the kitchen, holding out her hand to Max. "Give me your house keys."

"Why?"

"Because Darcy and Ginny are going to your place to see what they can find as proof your family was actually taken. If they find anything, it would help convince Rick and Vinnie to go to bat for you. Even if the local police aren't inclined to believe you, if they show up with evidence of a crime being committed, they'll have to investigate. Now, hand them over."

Max pulled a small keyring from his pocket attached to a bottle opener and handed it over. Maggie made a grabbing gesture at me. "Phone."

I handed it over and she put her brother's address into the map app. It was only a fifteen-minute drive. It hurt a little bit to know he lived so close to Brookhaven, and she had been apart from her brother for long enough that she had missed major changes in his life.

"Don't do anything until we get back," I told her. There was no need for Maggie to put herself in potential danger.

"I won't make a move without you." She leaned over and kissed me. "I have a feeling you're going to be my good luck charm."

Ginny plucked the keys from Maggie's hand and tugged on my arm. "Come on lucky. Let's go see what we can find."

Casting one last look at Maggie and her brother, I hurried out the front of the house. I was halfway to Ginny's car when I felt a presence on my shoulder. Beau nestled against the crook of my collarbone.

"We'll be fine, mate. You don't need to worry," I told him, pausing on the steps.

*'Extra protection.'*

"Guess we've got some extra magic on our side," I called ahead to Ginny as I descended the stairs and climbed into the passenger seat.

Ginny glanced at the reptile lounging on my shoulder. He shifted onto my left side, so he wouldn't be inconvenienced by the seatbelt. "Not a bad thing to go snooping in a potential crime scene without being seen."

"This was not how I expected my day to go," I admitted, securing the belt across my torso and hips.

"I hate to say it, but we were due for something like this. As much as I don't want to admit it, I think we all kind of live for solving the mysteries."

She nestled my phone in the center console where she could easily see it. Ginny revved the engine, pulling onto the street, and taking us out of Brookhaven. My pulse hammered in my veins as I tried not to let the worst case scenario fill my head with terrible images. We would know soon enough just how dire Chloe and Aneesa's situation truly was.

Worry settled in my gut, making every bump and pothole in the road jostle my belly. My celebration meal threatened to redecorate the interior of Ginny's car. She glanced at me as she pulled up at a stop sign about three minutes from Max's home.

"We're going to figure this out," she said in what I'm sure she thought was a reassuring tone. But it barely masked her own concern for Maggie and her family.

"I just don't want Maggie to get hurt in all of this." I studied my hands. "I don't know much about addiction, but I'm pretty sure the whole point of sobriety is to keep you away from temptation. What if this is too much for her?"

"Maggie is one of the strongest people I know, Darcy."

"Even strong people struggle, Ginny. Sometimes it's the strongest people who struggle the most because of the pressure they put on themselves to always be there for others. And I know this weighs on her since she feels like for so long her magic failed in helping the one person she really wanted to protect."

"Well, she's not doing this solo. We're here and she knows that. We aren't going to let her get sucked back into bad habits either."

She eased the car forward and in a matter of minutes we sat outside a squat three-floor apartment complex. I checked the address and noted that we were headed to the first floor. At least we didn't have far to go. Except Ginny didn't stop the car or even let it idle. Instead, she drove about a half block up from our destination before pulling down a side street that turned out to be a dead-end alley.

"What are you doing?"

"If we're planning to snoop around undetected, it doesn't make sense for us to be seen parking out front. I thought you understood all about sleuthing under the cover of camouflage."

Of course, she was right. I rubbed the sweat from my palms on the front of my pants before unbuckling my seatbelt. I was letting my concern for Maggie cloud my judgment. This wasn't the first potential crime scene I'd visited. I was by no means a professional, but I was at least somewhat seasoned at this point. Ginny climbed out of the car first, waving me on except I didn't move.

*'Not alone.'*

Beau's words in my head were all the reassurance I needed to join Ginny at the mouth of the alley. I didn't see any obvious signs of cameras in the area, but it was better to be safe than sorry. Ginny held up Max's apartment key. I took it from her, gripping it tight in my fist and held my other hand out to her. "It's easier on Beau if we have some point of contact first."

She slapped her hand into my waiting palm, and we laced our fingers together. I felt her give me a tiny squeeze as the strange feeling of Beau's magic rippled over us. It was always a mix of hot and cold sensations chasing each other over my body. It wasn't an unpleasant feeling, and one I could only truly associate with Beau sharing his invisibility magic with me.

Fully hidden from view now, Ginny and I walked down the street hand-in-hand until we came to a stop in front of Max's building. I studied the area. It didn't look particularly dangerous or prone to criminal activity. If the bookie had in fact snatched Chloe and Aneesa from the premises, someone should have noticed and called the police.

"Let's hope someone else is home, so the door doesn't magically open by itself," Ginny muttered as we approached the door.

I reached out and tried the handle. Locked. I spotted a call button on the side of the door. Just because they couldn't see us didn't mean we couldn't call a tenant, pretending to deliver something. Luckily, we didn't have to do that because a woman in workout clothes appeared through the small window in the door. She had earphones in, clearly not paying attention to her surroundings. I tugged Ginny back, so that we stood perpendicular to the door frame. The woman shoved the door open, letting it swing all the way open on her way out.

"Go!" I hissed, shoving Ginny forward while still holding hands as the door began its inward swing.

Somehow, we managed to slip through before it closed, and I let out a heavy breath. Only two units were housed on the first floor—one on either side of the stairs leading to the upper floors. I checked the key in my hand, finding a tiny 1B etched on the end of the keychain. The same 1B marked the entrance to our right. I slid the key into the lock and eased the door inward as quietly as possible.

The kitchen was a mess, just as Max had told us. Broken plates and bits of glass littered the ground. I noticed spilled baby formula pooling on the counter, leaving a large drip down the side of the sink. The door closed behind us and Beau's magic fell away.

"He wasn't kidding," Ginny noted, looking around the space.

"No, Max wasn't." Surveying the space, I didn't see much greenery. Maybe it was a long shot to think he had a green thumb and kept anything floral in the house.

"I'm going to check the other rooms," Ginny told me, peeling away from my side to disappear down a short hall. It ended with a door directly ahead, and another off to the right.

I stood in the ruined kitchen, trying to decide my next move. I didn't have to wait long though. A tiny voice sounded in my head, faint and timid, but very clearly a plant calling for my attention.

"Come on, now, don't be afraid. Just show me

where you are," I called softly to the still air around me.

A faint greenish light filtered across the kitchen to a spot behind a curtain in the window overlooking a side street. Doing my best not to leave more of a mess and avoiding the trail of broken glass, I danced my way across the kitchen and pushed the fabric aside to reveal a tiny sunflower stalk. Its leaves barely poked out above the dirt. The tiny plant trembled when I reached out to brush my fingertip across the surface of one of its leaves.

"You've seen something haven't you?" I murmured. "Please, I need to see."

*The plant trembled again, but my vision turned green. As I pivoted to face the empty kitchen, the scene rewound until I saw Chloe standing by the sink, preparing baby formula. Aneesa sat in a baby carrier on the woman's chest. I couldn't hear anything, but I could see the child's face bore an unhappy expression, her mouth open in a wail. An empty plate and glass sat on the counter. If I had to guess, she was planning to make her own meal after she'd tended to the baby. Chloe tried to rock the fussy infant as she prepared the bottle only to stop a moment later when the front door burst open. Two tall men appeared in the kitchen, and I could see bulges in their waistbands that couldn't be anything other than guns.*

*Chloe backed away from the intruders, her arms wrapped protectively around her daughter. They pointed at Chloe, and she shook her head. The plant couldn't understand language but it could could convey her fear. One of the men swiped his hand at the plate, sending it and the glass shattering to the floor. The formula toppled over, spilling on the counter and into the sink. The second brute pushed in and grabbed Chloe by the arm, dragging her out of view. The first man moved to the table where he hastily scribbled a note. I assumed that it was the one Max had described.*

*Moments later, the second man appeared with Chloe in tow, a diaper bag gripped in one meaty hand. Well, that likely explained the clothes left in disarray if he had forced her to hastily pack for the baby. My stomach lurched as they dragged her from the apartment, the baby screaming all the while, drowning out her mother's own protests. I could make out a bruise on her cheek and her eyes appeared puffy from crying.*

"Darcy?" Ginny's voice rang through the small space, pulling me from the plant's memory.

"Max was telling the truth. Two guys with guns burst in and took Chloe and the baby. They broke the dishes and I'm guessing forced her to grab some clothes for her and the baby before they dragged her out," I reported as Ginny came back into view.

"Yeah, that seems to fit with what I found in the bedroom. Come on, let's go back to Tania's and pull in Rick and Vinnie. We've got enough at least to file a missing person's report and get the search going."

We got to the unit's entrance and Beau cloaked all of us once more. I flipped the lock before we eased the door shut and retreated to the front of the building. Our hope that we'd run into another resident coming in or exiting when we needed to leave was too much to ask of the universe. We were just going to have to risk it.

Ginny gripped my hand and nudged the front door open just enough for us to squeeze out. I didn't exhale until we had made it down the street and out of sight. We hurried to her car, and she only let go of my hand when she opened the driver side door. I sprinted around the front of the car and climbed in beside her.

"I'm going to text Maggie and let her know we're on our way back."

Ginny put the B&B's address into her phone, following the map directions she executed a very illegal U-turn in the middle of the alley. I pulled up my messages with Maggie and sent her a quick text.

The trip back to Brookhaven seemed to take forever. I scanned our surroundings, hoping that every turn we made would be onto Main Street and the familiar surroundings of home. When we finally pulled into the driveway at the B&B, I practically tumbled from the passenger seat in my haste to exit the vehicle. Rick's squad car sat out front, too. I hadn't seen it on our departure.

When we walked through the foyer, I caught Sam floating partway up the stairs looking genuinely worried. I moved into the kitchen to hear the dishwasher running, but the space was vacant. Making the circuit through the dining room, I ended up in the living room. Maggie sat beside Max with a laptop perched on her knees. Rick occupied one of the other chairs, pen and paper in hand. The expression on his face was all business.

"You and your wife were on good terms?" Rick waited for Max's answer.

"Yeah. I told you already, I didn't do anything to her. You have to believe me."

Rick glanced my way as my footsteps betrayed my arrival. "I saw what happened. Max was nowhere near the place. Two armed men broke into the apartment. They forced Chloe and the baby to leave with them," I explained. "They're in real danger."

Maggie's fingers tapped steadily on the computer. "Then it's a good thing I remembered my password."

"You don't have to use your own money. Please, let me give it to you," Max begged her. "I have enough to cover the buy-in."

"I know you do. But if I'm going to do this, it's going to be my way. And that means I play with my own money."

Without warning, Max wrapped his sister in a sideways embrace, burying his head into her shoulder. She awkwardly patted his knee. "I'm sorry we fell out of touch for so long, but I'm going to get your family back. You have my word."

"I know you said that the police didn't believe it when you tried to report this to them and that they blamed you. But can you think of any other reason they would have to not investigate Tony? I mean, do they owe him debts too?" I settled on Maggie's other side, trying to follow what she was doing on the computer.

The screen displayed a flurry of activity with notifications that she'd been accepted to the tournament and provided links to the different brackets. It all looked like gibberish to me.

"The sheriff is Tony's cousin. It wouldn't surprise me if he owed Tony some money, too. But there's no way the Sheriff is going against his own family."

His announcement made my mouth dry, and my stomach performed an uncomfortable flip. Would we run into deliberate interference from a corrupt lawman if we tried to do more digging? Would they push back against Rick if he went looking? A shiver that had nothing to do with the temperature ran down my spine, causing goosebumps to prickle along my arms.

"So, what do we do now?"

"Now, I'll start doing what I used to be really good at," Maggie answered, showing me the computer screen where a virtual poker hand sat on the lower half of the screen. In real time, digital cards disappeared and flipped over. I noted that the bet for the game was already over $1,000. As I watched, it ticked up to $1,500.

"Can you really match that?" My voice betrayed my own inexperience, cracking at the end of the question.

"I am going to be fine, Darcy."

"In the meantime, I'm going to try and put a little

collegial pressure on the sheriff to actually take the report seriously," Rick noted, standing as he spoke. "Darcy, do you happen to have a good recollection of what the men looked like?"

"Uh, I mean they were both tall. Dark hair, white blokes, armed, but I didn't see them actually pull their weapons. I think the threat that they even existed was enough to make Chloe comply."

"If I manage to find a photo array of Tony's known associates, I'll bring it by."

"Happy to do whatever I can to help," I said. As it was, I felt pretty bloody useless next to Maggie as she focused intently on the game.

"Max, I'm going to recommend you stick around town for the duration, especially if no one went over the scene properly," Rick continued.

"I can do that," Max answered, his gaze not leaving the screen in Maggie's lap.

"I will get a room made up for you," Tania said as she stepped into the room carrying a tray of coffee mugs and a small pitcher of cream.

"I'll pay you what I can."

"Nonsense. You are *familia*. You are going to stay here as our guest, because you need the help."

Just then, Maggie yelled a triumphant, "Yes!" and fist pumped the air as the card hand closed. The screen showed she was up almost $2,000 already. Maybe this part of the plan would be all over in a matter of hours, and I wouldn't have to worry about Maggie's safety. Or this could just be the start of a dangerous path we would have to walk together. Either way, I wasn't about to let her go. So, I leaned over and planted a kiss on her cheek.

"Bring them home."

**6**

*I* dreamt of playing cards dancing through the room around me, racing past at such speed I could hardly make sense of them before they vanished. I woke; the sheets matted to my body by cold sweat. The other side of the mattress was empty. Maggie had come to bed with me a little after ten the night before. The tournament had concluded for the day, and she'd advanced several brackets, banking nearly half of what Max owed Tony. My heart hammered against my ribs as I struggled to free myself from the sheets. My phone read a little after three in the morning.

"Maggie?" I called in a stage whisper as I stepped into the hallway.

Silence answered me.

Where was Sam when I needed him? Or Beau? Both of my usual supernatural co-conspirators were conspicuously absent. I tip-toed down the hall to the top of the stairs. Closing my eyes, I took a deep breath, convincing myself not to panic. As I touched the smooth surface of the wall to my left and the contoured wood of the railing to my right, a hazy greenish vision popped into my mind's eye. I saw Maggie hunched over a laptop in the dining room, an empty mug beside her. With the green filter the light from the computer screen gave her an unearthly appearance.

Releasing a sharp exhale, the world came back to me darkened by the night. I hadn't intended to use my magic to track down my girlfriend. Yet that's exactly what happened. I even knew which plant had given me the vantage point. Quietly, I moved down the stairs. Max had taken one of the empty rooms down the hall and I didn't want to wake him. He needed sleep more than the rest of us. I'd tried to pretend I hadn't heard Maggie insisting he take some of her chamomile tea to bed with him. I was almost certain she'd won that argument, and the drink had knocked him out.

Once I reached the landing on the first floor and listened intently, picking up the soft click-clack of fingers against keys in the distance. The plants had shown me Maggie's current location after all. I hurried through the foyer and kitchen.

"Thanks for letting me know Maggie is okay," I whispered to the plants sitting in the darkened space. I reached out as I walked into the dining room and brushed the tips of my fingers against the soft leaves of the flower sitting by the window.

My girlfriend still sat in front of her laptop, staring at the screen. She was so consumed by whatever she'd found she hadn't heard me enter. I didn't want to frighten her. I cleared my throat as loud as possible and made a show of pulling out one of the chairs at the end of the table nearest the kitchen as loudly as I could.

"I thought the tournament was over for the day," I said, finally drawing her attention.

Dark circles ringed her eyes, her cheeks were pale and her short, red hair stuck up at odd angles. She looked even more exhausted after she dragged her fingers through her messy mop and rubbed her eyes. "It did. I was just ... I don't know, honestly ..."

I pulled the chair around to sit beside her, so I had a better vantage point for the computer screen. She had opened an online betting site and it didn't appear to have any connection to the tournament she'd entered the day before. "I thought things were going well in the tournament."

"They are, but that's the thing about gambling. It's not guaranteed. You can hit a losing streak just as fast as you land on a winner. I was, uh ... maybe trying to figure out a way to diversify my chances of getting Max the money."

"Do you think that's a good idea? I mean ... I don't want to tell you what to do, but this doesn't seem like you."

"I know you are worried about me, Darcy. And I love you for that, more than I can put into words. But from what you described to Rick and Vinnie, these guys are serious. And my sister-in-law and niece could be in real trouble."

"Rick and Vinnie are working on finding them. That's what they do. We have to be okay with them taking those risks, right?"

Maggie let out a soft snort of laughter. "I don't think either of us believe that you aren't going to rush off at the first hint that you can help make a difference, even if you really shouldn't."

"I'm trying not to be a reckless hero. But, if it meant protecting you and the people you love, I'd do it in a heartbeat."

I reached over and closed the laptop. "I don't

think going deeper down the rabbit hole is going to end up how either of us wants. You did well yesterday, and I have to believe that you're going to do well in the next round, too. Besides, can't you just cash out once you've earned what you need?"

Maggie shook her head. "No. I was reading the rules again after I got up. You're in it until the end and only get any money if you win in the final bracket."

"How long's that from where you're at now?"

"Honestly, too far."

"What if we went looking for Tony? I'm pretty sure you can be the scary big sister and I've taken down my fair share of wannabe thugs with my magic."

"There's that impulsiveness I was expecting," she teased. "But really, I don't think us going after Tony is the right move. We could just scare him. Besides, people think I'm playing as Max. If I showed up, things could get very bad for my brother."

"In that case, maybe we can go back to bed? You might be able to take the day off work, but Sage is expecting me for the morning shift," I said through a poorly stifled yawn.

"Of course."

I pulled Maggie to her feet and didn't let go of

her hand until we were back upstairs in my room. I snuggled against the warmth of her body beneath the blankets.

SIX THIRTY CAME FAR TOO QUICKLY and I let out a groan as my phone blared at me to get up. Maggie still slept beside me, and I did my best to extricate myself without waking her. At least she'd stayed put after her half-hearted attempt to spread her gambling wings beyond the tournament. I grabbed a brief shower and dressed for work before taking the stairs two at a time to find Tania seated at the kitchen table with a teacup in hand.

"I am sorry, Darcy. I wasn't in the mood to make anything this morning," she confessed, glancing at the barren stove.

"I understand. It has to be overwhelming trying to sort through Maggie's and Max's emotions. It must be pure chaos for you. I wish I could do something to help."

"Looking for Max's missing family is enough."

"I'll stop by Ginny's café and grab something on my way to High Time," I answered. "I know you'll do it anyway, but could you keep an eye on Maggie and

Max today? I'm worried about them both ... that they might do something they'll regret out of desperation."

"Of course, I will."

I gave her a wave and an appreciative smile before I headed for the front of the B&B. The walk to Ginny's was brief and I was grateful to find the café open. Ginny sat at the counter with one of her oversized mugs brimming with coffee. I settled in beside her.

"Surprised you're here for breakfast," she noted without looking at me. She slid the mug in my direction and pushed off the seat at the counter. She rounded it, produced another mug and a half-full pot, and poured herself a fresh cup.

"Tania wasn't really up for making breakfast today," I answered. "With everything going on with Maggie and Max, I can't blame her."

"How are they holding up?"

"Max was still sleeping, courtesy of Maggie's chamomile tea. And she was up in the wee hours looking for other ways to get the money he needs to pay off his debt."

"I'm sorry."

"It's fine. She didn't end up placing any bets. But I won't lie, it did have me worried for a minute." I took a sip from the large mug and savored the sharp flavor of the coffee. "I still can't believe the police in Max's town wouldn't even take his complaint seriously."

"Rick told me last night that he filed a request for a search warrant to dust for prints and everything at Max's place. He's had to get creative with asserting jurisdiction, but at least he's trying."

"I know Max will be grateful for it." Ginny disappeared momentarily into the kitchen, returning with a plate of eggs and toast with a side of strawberry jam. As if she'd been expecting someone to turn up after all. "Can't go to work on an empty stomach," she noted when I arched a brow at her.

"Thanks." I accepted the food and turned my attention to eating. I was due at work soon and didn't need to be late. "I wish the plant at Max's place had been able to show me where those thugs had taken Chloe and the baby."

"That would be too easy," Ginny answered with a snort. "You have magic, and it's served you well. But it isn't a cure-all and doesn't give you the answers on command."

"Don't I know it."

"Just don't go too far, Darcy. Maggie would never forgive any of us if something happened to you."

"I don't plan on being the hero," I replied.

Yet, I couldn't shake the feeling that if it came down to it, I'd jump in front of danger to protect Maggie and her family. I wanted to believe it was simply because it was the right thing to do. But a part of me I hadn't entirely given voice to until now reminded me that they could be my family one day, too. If she'd have me.

"You better get going. Don't want to be late to work," Ginny said, as if reading my earlier thoughts. I reached for my wallet, and she waved me off. "No need to pay. Those eggs came out a little dodgy and I can always say you were my taste tester."

"You know, charity is good and all. But if you keep giving things away, you're going to go out of business."

"Oh please, people love me enough to keep coming here and spending their money. I can afford to give out a free meal now and again."

"If you see Maggie, can you just check in on her?" I knew I'd made the same request of Tania. Yet I couldn't help but feel overprotective of my girlfriend.

"Sure."

"Cheers."

Before I could go, she poured the coffee into a

large to-go cup and handed it over. "Something tells me you're going to need all the fuel you can get."

I downed most of it before I had even reached the employee entrance to High Time a few minutes later. In hindsight, it probably wasn't the wisest move as the caffeine hit me in a wild rush, making my nerve endings buzz. The extra boost wouldn't last for long, and I could feel the oncoming edge of the crash looming even as I tended the plants around me. The usual peace and quiet of the grow room was stifling today.

Every few minutes, I found myself checking my phone in the hopes Maggie had texted saying everything was over and Max's family had been returned. The screen remained devoid of incoming texts or voicemails. By the time my phone read ten o'clock, my head was swimming with equal parts caffeine crash and worry over Maggie. I should have heard something by now. Even if it was just an update on her position in the tournament.

"Darcy, everything okay?" Sage's question caught me off guard as I realized I'd been staring at a spot on the wall opposite me without really seeing it. My hands were knuckle deep in soil, but the plant between my fingers sat unresponsive and limp.

"Sorry, I don't know if I'm feeling very well," I

admitted. It was technically true. My boss didn't need to know everything going on with Maggie.

"Bit too much excitement yesterday?"

"Something like that. I hate to beg off work, but I'm not sure I'm going to be much good for the plants today."

"Why don't you take the day and get some rest? We can manage the afternoon without you," she replied.

"You're sure?"

"Go home. We will be fine."

I pulled my fingers from the soil, brushing the bits that clung to my fingertips off on the edge of the table. After retrieving my belongings from my locker, I started the walk back to the B&B.

I made it as far as the front steps when the door opened and Maggie appeared, eyes wide. "I was just about to call you."

"What's happened?"

"It's easier if I show you."

I followed her inside to the dining room. Her laptop sat in the same spot it had occupied earlier. The tournament page sat open, but no game play was happening on screen. Instead, a message displayed what appeared to be a private chat. There was no username that I could make out. But the message was clear.

**The people you're looking for aren't the only ones missing. If you aren't fast, they'll disappear forever, and they won't even know they're gone.**

"What's that supposed to mean? And who is this even from?"

"I was waiting for the next round of the tournament to start, and someone messaged me with this. They've managed to hide their identity and information, which I don't even know how they'd do it unless they're familiar with the tournament's software. And that raises even more questions. But they know that Max is missing family? That's problematic on an entirely different level."

"Write back, and ask what they're talking about," I urged.

Maggie sat down and typed out a message.

**How will they not remember they're missing? And how do you know I'm looking for anyone?**

The message sat unanswered for a good two or three minutes before a reply came.

It's how the game is played. They fall under a spell and then they're gone. And everyone has someone they're looking for. It's the price of admission.

Maggie and I exchanged a look. "Do you think they mean a literal spell?" My question came out as a rasp.

"Either way, we have more incentive to get to the final round and beat the house."

Things just got a whole lot more complicated.

7

"**I** think we ought to show this to Rick," I said, pointing to the message string still on the screen.

"I don't know what he'd be able to do about it. I have no idea who sent it. There's no name on the messages and we can't even be sure it's someone playing in the tournament," Maggie countered.

Before I could point out that between her and her brother, they had a decent chance of tracing the message sender with their combined hacking skills, Max appeared in the dining room. He looked more rested than when he'd arrived the day before.

"What's going on?"

"It looks like someone thinks more people than just Chloe and the baby have been taken," Maggie answered solemnly. "And maybe there's some sort of magic involved."

"Magic? How?"

"All we got was a hint about some spell, and the taken forget everything ... but we don't really have anything beyond that," I interjected. "We were going to take the information to Chief Hayes and see if there's anything the department can do, maybe track the IP address or something."

"Is that a good idea? I mean, telling the chief of police about magic?"

I couldn't keep the snort from escaping my lips. Max gave me a confused look. "Sorry, I forgot you don't live here. It's become pretty common knowledge around here. The chief can turn into a giant cougar. So, magic isn't really a taboo topic around him. Or his deputy."

"If you think it could help, tell them everything."

Beside me, Maggie's phone buzzed with an incoming call from the clinic's main line. "Give me a minute."

She scooped up the device and stepped into the living room before answering the call. Max sunk into her vacant seat and stared at the screen, brow furrowed. An awkward silence fell over the room in Maggie's absence as I studied the man before me. He might have gotten much-needed sleep, but I could still see circles under his eyes and the paleness in his cheeks. I noticed that his hair was actually longer and shaggier than Maggie's but the same auburn hue. They also had the same beautiful blue eyes.

"She's up more than I thought she'd be," he said offhandedly, scrolling through the tournament brackets.

"You know, she was researching other ways to get the money this morning."

He swiveled to face me. "Please tell me she didn't."

"I stopped her. Well, I mean ... she stopped herself ..." I took a breath before adding, "I hope you didn't take that as accusatory."

"I wouldn't blame you if it was. I walked back into her life and dumped this drama at her feet. And she took it and ran with it." He glanced towards the living room before adding. "I know she feels guilty she couldn't fix me."

"She is just trying to protect her family. And you don't need fixing."

He laughed. "Yeah, I do. I'm an addict. I know it, and she knew it. She saw it before I'd even placed my first bet. I remember watching her play and getting this rush every time she won. I kept thinking, if I got that feeling watching her play, how much better would it be if I was winning."

"Even still, you are working on your sobriety. That's something you've done all on your own. You didn't need her to fix anything." Our trip to Vinnie's uncle's racetrack flashed through my mind. The unease Maggie had displayed being there. The fear that her brother would be there, losing money with bad bets. "Can I ask you something?"

"Sure."

"You obviously know about magic. I mean, Maggie is a healer after all. But ... and I don't mean to be impolite or critical ... I don't really get much magic vibe from you."

"Yeah, that's because I'm not magical." He let out a soft, somber laugh. "If it weren't for the fact that Maggie and I look so much alike, I'd have asked my parents if she was adopted. They don't have magic, either. She's the outlier."

"I know how that feels," I said. We'd been together over eighteen months, and I hadn't realized we'd both come from non-magical parents. Clearly, magic was somewhere in her bloodline. "It must have been hard for everyone growing up."

"She put a lot of pressure on herself, that's for sure. What about you?"

"I only realized I had magic a couple years ago. It didn't really go over well with my parents, which is how I ended up here. But I'm glad it happened the way it did. I wouldn't have met everyone in Brookhaven. I wouldn't have found where I belong otherwise."

Before Max could respond, Maggie walked back in. "I have to run to the clinic for an emergency patient. I'll be back as fast as I can." She checked the time. "The tournament shouldn't be starting again for a while."

"Go be the hero, Magpie," Max said, shooing her off.

"Don't worry, I'll keep an eye on him," I assured her and patted her brother's shoulder.

She'd just disappeared into the kitchen when I pulled out my phone and called Vinnie. He picked up on the second ring. "Darcy, everything okay?"

"Can you or Rick come by Tania's? Maggie was sent some weird messages through the tournament platform that I think you ought to see."

"Sure. I can swing by. Give me ten minutes."

"Huh, so you two do this often? Solving the mystery and saving the day?"

"I wouldn't say often, but it's probably a more regular thing for us than most people. I swear we don't try to get stuck in the middle of messes. It just sort of happens."

"Well, like I said yesterday ... I'm glad you do, because I wouldn't trust anyone else to get my family back."

"I understand why you didn't trust the local authorities to look into this for you, but doesn't this seem like a bit of a strange escalation? I mean, why would Tony suddenly become so violent?"

"I don't know. He threatened my family, then I came home, and they were gone."

"Darcy?" Vinnie's voice rang out from the front of the B&B.

"In the dining room," I answered.

A moment later, the deputy appeared, pen and paper at the ready, along with his phone. "So, what happened?"

Max moved to the next chair over, allowing Vinnie to take the seat in front of Maggie's laptop. He studied the screen and arched a brow before looking at me. "I definitely ought to loop the chief in on this."

"Is there anything you can do to track who sent the messages?"

"I'd need to take Maggie's laptop, and something

tells me that she's not going to let us do that until she's done with this whole thing."

"I mean, I might be able to look into the coding," Max offered, but Vinnie shook his head. "Or log into the site on a different computer and see if it's still there."

"You're the victim of the crime, Max," Vinnie noted. "You can't go snooping through things. Especially if it involves doing illegal activity."

Max opened his mouth to protest when a notification pinged on the screen, drawing our collective attention. An animated envelope appeared, opening to reveal a full-page invitation to an exclusive event tonight at ten o'clock with the ability to bring a plus one.

I glanced at Max. "Is this normal?"

"No, nothing like this happened during a tournament before. I mean, not that I've ever made it as far as Maggie's done. But even still, you sort of get to know people. They talk, and I've never heard of something like this."

"So, Tony isn't prone to hosting extravagant parties," Vinnie noted mostly to himself, jotting down the details from the invitation. "You know, we haven't been able to actually find Tony. Any idea where he might be hiding out?"

"Believe me, if I knew where he was skulking, I'd be busting down his door," Max answered darkly. "Not that I'm admitting to anything ... illegal or otherwise to a cop."

"What do we do about it? I mean, if everyone thinks Max is the one still playing, Maggie showing up would be suspicious," I noted.

"What would be suspicious?" Maggie's voice came from my right, making me jump.

"I thought you'd gone to the clinic," I said, realizing too late that my words carried an annoyed tone.

"I was halfway there and got a call that things had sorted themselves out. I've clearly missed something."

"See for yourself," Vinnie answered and took a step back from the table.

Maggie filled the vacated space and studied the screen. "Since when do online gamblers meet up in person?"

"They don't," Max answered. "Something feels off about this."

"The fact your family's been kidnapped essentially for ransom seems off to begin with," Maggie muttered. "Well, it would be rude to decline the invitation."

"You can't be serious," Vinnie scoffed.

"Like hell I am. These people took my family. They aren't going to get away with it. And if we're lucky, maybe we'll find Chloe and the baby at the event."

"Only problem is people will be expecting me."

"Oh come on, Max, you can't possibly know most of the people who would be showing up."

"I could if Tony's running things," her brother argued.

Maggie bent over the keyboard, her fingers flying. The invitation minimized and another window on the screen popped up, filling with strings of characters and symbols I had no hope of understanding. "This went out to every player still in the tournament. At least thirty or forty people are being asked to attend. You can't know all of them. And besides, even if you told some of them your name was Max, that could be short for Maxine—"

"I don't like this at all," Vinnie interrupted.

I didn't either.

But the glint in my girlfriend's eye told me there was no arguing with her. She was going to the event whether we were there to have her back or not. The way Vinnie's shoulders slumped, he clearly came to the same conclusion a moment later.

"At least let us set up some surveillance, so you aren't going in alone. As Rick would tell you if he were here, you aren't police. You don't have training."

I looked at Maggie. "Vinnie makes a good point. If we're going to be undercover, we should at least give the police a solid chance to gather evidence with surveillance."

"We, huh?" Maggie arched a brow at me.

"You didn't think I'd let you go in solo, did you?" I leaned over and kissed her. "Where you go, I go."

"Okay. Well then I suppose we better get ready." She brought the invite back up on screen. "I guess we better find some fancy attire to attend this soiree."

"I'm going to loop Rick in and see what we can set up ahead of time. And don't be surprised if he throws a fit about you two going in at all," Vinnie warned before turning his attention to Max. "I really need you to think of any place Tony might go. I've put a call in to the sheriff in your town. Maybe they can shed some light on what might have prompted Tony to go from simply being a bookie to orchestrating kidnapping."

"I told you, they're family. They aren't going to do anything."

"Maybe not, but I had to try anyway. And we're

going to need you along to help us identify people on scene."

Max looked less than enthused about the prospect of spending his evening in police company. "Okay, fine."

"We'll be back to pick you up an hour before the event," Vinnie announced before pocketing his notepad and pen, and heading for the front door.

"Looks like the tournament is getting ready to kick off again," Maggie announced as she sat back down. I looked over her shoulder, noting a tiny banner running across the top of the screen. It proclaimed that the tournament would be temporarily suspended later to allow time for the in-person event.

"I'll see what I can find for you to wear," I told Maggie before leaving her and Max in the dining room.

I was halfway upstairs when Sam materialized ahead of me, protruding out of the riser from the ankle up. "You're headed to some creepy, yet fancy party, right? Hmm ... you don't have anything worth wearing."

"Thanks, mate. That's really helpful," I deadpanned.

"Tania has some things stashed away in her

closet that might fit you both and make you presentable."

"Did I hear you volunteering my closet?" Tania called, stepping out of the bathroom.

"You are the keeper of the sparkly dresses," Sam answered with a dramatic bow.

"I don't want to stand out," I squeaked, feeling suddenly self-conscious. "If anything, Maggie should be the one people focus on, not me."

"Don't worry. I have something I think might work. Come."

Tania waved for me to come up the rest of the stairs and I followed her into the master bedroom. She opened a closet door I hadn't noticed before and rummaged through the contents for a few minutes before pulling out a dark, forest green knee-length dress with three-quarter length sleeves.

"Try this."

Sam gave me an expectant look as Tania held out the fabric. I made a spinning gesture. "Turn around."

"Not like I'm interested in what you've got," Sam muttered, but he turned his back to me.

I discarded my work clothes and pulled the dress on. The fabric cascaded over my curves in all the right ways. I turned to the full-length mirror in the corner.

"Damn, you are going to knock 'em dead when they do notice you," Sam exclaimed, letting out an accompanying whistle.

The green complimented my coloring and gave me an elegant look. It was still subdued enough that in the right setting, I could get by unnoticed. Just what I needed for reconnaissance.

"*Perfecto*," Tania gushed with a smile from over my left shoulder.

"It really is," I agreed, turning back to face my friend. "Where'd you get it?"

"From time to time, people leave things behind. The nicer things, items that other people might need one day, I keep. The rest, I donate to charity."

"Got something in there for Maggie?"

Tania pivoted back to the closet before pulling out a sexy black dress. Yeah, that would work.

"All of this feels just so strange," I noted as I sat at the foot of the bed. "Why announce an in-person event? Why bring all these unknown people together when everything is usually kept online?"

"There are far more questions than answers right now. But my gut tells me you are on the right path to finding the answers, along with Max's wife and daughter."

It still felt like a bizarre turn of events, especially

for someone who'd gone to great lengths to abduct a woman and her baby, just to collect on a gambling debt. Surely having Max or Maggie playing in the tournament for as long as possible was the better plan of attack. Tonight, we'd know for certain what was going on. We just had to hope Maggie's winning streak lasted long enough to get us through the front door.

8

*J*ust before ten o'clock at night, I sat beside Maggie in the front passenger seat of her car with Rick's civilian car parked a dozen rows away from us. She had donned the sexy little black dress from Tania's closet and looked absolutely stunning. Yet there was a steeliness about her demeanor that made me nervous. My anxiety was on high alert as I secured the tiny earpiece Rick had given us before leaving Tania's B&B.

Maggie secured her own earpiece and asked, "You have any last suggestions before we go inside?"

"Yeah, let the professionals handle this," Rick said in both of our ears.

"Boss, we don't have probable cause to be in

there yet. Nothing illegal is happening from the outside, so us showing up in uniform wouldn't be appropriate." Vinnie's voice came over the comms in response.

"They aren't trained for this," Rick argued.

"But we're willing to take the risk. Besides, it's my family they're holding hostage," Maggie retorted.

"And you're our family," Rick muttered.

"We are going to be as careful as we can be," I said louder than I would have given the confines of the car. But I wanted to be sure they heard me.

"Just talk normally and it should pick up your voice," Vinnie reminded me. "Even if it's noisy in there, these comms are supposed to be pretty good, and we've set them to record everything you hear and say. If you see Tony, try to get him to talk, and possibly explain why he's resorted to such drastic measures to collect on his debts."

"I'll do what I can," I promised, but there was no way I'd just happen upon Max's bookie. The universe wasn't that forgiving.

Out of the corner of my eye, I watched Maggie adjust her dress and brush a few strands of loose hair out of her eyes. Her steeliness was slipping now that we were about to walk into an unknown situation. We both exited her car, and I rounded the hood of the car to reach for her hand. "We've got this. And if anything starts to feel off, we can just leave."

"Let's hope that's true," she said darkly.

We were halfway to the entrance when I felt my phone buzz in the clutch Tania had dug out of her closet for me to borrow. I pulled it out to see Tania's number flashing on the screen. "Hi, Tania. We're about to head in."

"Would you wait one minute?"

"Uh, sorry?" It sounded as if she was talking to someone else.

"Darcy, don't go inside yet."

"Why not?"

"Beau wants to be there with you. Just as a precaution."

I wasn't above having my chameleon friend on hand in case either Maggie or I needed to get around unseen. "Uh, sure."

"He should be there soon."

Even after all the time I'd lived in Brookhaven and been privy to Beau's magic, I still didn't entirely understand his ability to move around town so effortlessly for a tiny reptile. I ended the call and stowed my phone again. Just as I was about to fill Rick and Vinnie in on the change in plan, the engine of a motorcycle revved in the distance. It grew louder until an unknown figure appeared, speeding towards us. The rider stopped just short of the back of Maggie's car and tugged off their helmet.

"Ginny, how did she get my bike?" Vinnie demanded through my earpiece.

"Is that Vinnie's?" I translated, given she couldn't hear his annoyed mutterings over the earpiece.

"He shouldn't leave it parked behind the cafe with the keys in it," she answered with a smirk before patting the empty air above the seat behind her. With a shimmer, Beau appeared.

*'Here to help.'*

He disappeared before the thought finished playing out in my mind so as not to be noticed on any video surveillance. I smiled at his words and scooped him up, positioning him in his favorite perch on my shoulder. He rippled and blended in with the forest green of my dress.

Ginny's own phone rang. I could hear Rick chide her over the line. "Next time, ask before you borrow other people's vehicles."

She just rolled her eyes at his admonishment, donned the helmet, and took off on the motorcycle. Vinnie continued muttering under his breath for a moment longer before turning his focus back to

Maggie and me. "Why exactly do you need a magical lizard?"

"The message we got suggested that magic is being used. Better to combat like with like," Maggie replied before grabbing my left wrist. "We better get inside."

As we stepped inside, I did my best to take in the interior surroundings, committing what details I could to memory. The building itself looked as if it were part of a larger complex. Perhaps it had been retail shops at one point. It now appeared as if it had been converted into a large single space with dim lighting and far too heavy air conditioning. A slender woman stood at the inside door with a fistful of wristbands. When she looked at us, her eyes looked a bit glazed over. As if she'd been sleep deprived or maybe gone through some sort of drug withdrawal.

"Username?" she asked, monotone.

Maggie offered up her brother's username. The woman glanced down at a clipboard then back up at Maggie.

"Wrist," she said in the same monotone.

Maggie and I did as requested, and she secured the bands around our right wrists. I half expected her to say more, or at the very least give us instructions on what we should do when we got past her. She just stared ahead in silence. Maggie pulled the heavy door in front of us open, and we walked inside.

Where the entryway had been far too cold and dim, the inside space was so loud I couldn't even hear myself think. Small, high tables were dotted throughout the room and people milled about with drinks in hand.

"Could they have just decided to throw a party?" I asked, hoping Maggie could still hear me.

"Maybe." Maggie pulled out her own phone and sent off a text I couldn't read. A moment later, she got a reply. Showing me the screen, she explained, "That's Tony. We find him, and hopefully we find Chloe and the baby."

"I'm on it." Not that I didn't trust my girlfriend to have a civil conversation with the man, but I also knew that he'd messed with her family and that brought out her overprotectiveness. A server in a black vest and dark red shirt appeared carrying a tray of champagne flutes. Maggie plucked two from the tray and before she walked off, handed me one. "Blend in."

"Right." After a beat I added, "All of these people

are bloody good at poker. But I know nothing. What am I supposed to talk about?"

"You've got Beau. Use him."

With that, she disappeared into the crowd, leaving me standing there solo. My phone buzzed in my clutch, and I pulled it out to find she'd at least sent me Tony's photo. Right, time to go looking. The noise, which didn't seem like it should be possible given the number of people here, was overwhelming, even as I moved to the periphery of the room. My head throbbed as I tried to find a quieter spot to stand and observe the room.

"What do you see?" Rick's voice came through the earpiece.

"Just people mingling around little tables. No sign of Tony. Maggie's gone off to mingle and talk poker. I'm just ... trying not to have my head explode from all the noise."

"You can do this." The words of encouragement from Rick were a bit of a surprise, but a welcome one. We'd come a long way since our early days, but it still felt strange to have him be so supportive of my involvement in a case.

I took a few deep breaths and started walking the perimeter, briefly scanning the face of every man I came across, hoping to find Tony. He wasn't on this side of the room though. My heart hammered a little more as I turned the corner and nearly collided with one of the servers carrying an almost empty tray. The glass of champagne I'd forgotten about in my left hand sloshed, dampening the front of my dress.

"Oh, bugger!"

The server—a young woman who couldn't have been old enough to be serving the drinks on hand—looked embarrassed, ducking her head. "Sorry, miss."

"No, it's my fault. I wasn't watching where I was going."

"I've ruined your dress."

"Maybe there's a restroom or something where I could get cleaned up?"

The server looked around the space before lowering her voice, so I could hardly hear her. "Come with me."

Before I could ask where we were headed, she grabbed my hand and pulled me along, leading me through a door marked, 'Staff Only' and down a long brightly lit corridor. By the time my eyes had adjusted to the difference in lighting, she'd taken me into a kitchen which appeared to be long dormant. It must have been the last vestiges of a restaurant. I could see a thick coat of dust covering the appliances and countertops. But the young woman ran a towel under the tap, heaving a sigh of relief when water spurted out of the pipes and turned to hand it to me.

"How'd you know this was back here?" I dabbed at the dress, doing my best not to bump Beau's tail that hung down on the front of my dress. "It seems a bit unused."

"I ... I don't know," she admitted, still not meeting my gaze.

"I don't mean to pry, but you seem a bit young to be serving alcohol, even for a private event."

Her jaw worked, as if she were choosing her words carefully. When she finally looked up at me, she had that same glazed look as the woman handing out wristbands at the entrance. "I ... I think I am?"

"Darcy, you need to get back out there and find Tony. He's the one we're after." Vinnie's voice filled my ear.

I bit down on my lip for a moment to keep from responding to his words. "You know, I'm supposed to be meeting a friend here. A bloke called Tony. Do you know where I could find him?"

"I don't know anyone named Tony."

I pulled out my phone and showed her the photo

sent by Maggie. "That's him. Maybe you've seen him around?"

She studied the photo and some of the glazed over expression vanished for a moment. "I think I saw him by the bar."

"Brilliant." I set the towel down on the counter, leaving a clear trail in the dust and grime. "Maybe you could show me? I honestly haven't made it that far into the room yet. It's rather massive out there."

"Yeah. Okay."

The girl led me back the way we'd come and as we were about to leave the kitchen behind, Beau's voice echoed in my head.

*'Look right.'*

I turned the direction he'd instructed and spotted something protruding from one of the center islands on the floor. I bent down and pulled it out—a baby's pacifier. I secreted it in my clutch before following the server along the corridor. I sucked in a deep breath as we stepped into the main area and the light shifted to a darker ambiance. The sound was as cacophonous as before and it made my temples throb. But I followed my guide around the perimeter of the room to a long high-top bar. She gestured to a man who stood a few feet away downing shots.

"Think I might have found Tony," I said under my breath. I scanned the room, hoping I'd catch a glimpse of Maggie. "What about Maggie?"

"Rick's got her. Just try to strike up a conversation with Tony as casually as you can," Vinnie answered in my ear.

"By the way I found something in the back kitchen that I think you're going to be interested in."

"Tony first."

I squared my shoulders and sidled up to the bar just as Tony spun to face me. My hope that I'd get a straight answer out of the man dwindled sharply as I took in his beet red complexion, sweaty cheeks, and bloodshot eyes. He'd clearly been drinking for some time and didn't appear as if he could hold his liquor well.

"Tony?"

"Do I know you?" He surprisingly didn't slur his words.

"I'm a friend of Max Henley," I answered. "You remember Max, yeah? Guy who's trying to turn his life around and support his family. And you decided it would be a grand idea to send in your thugs and kidnap his wife and baby girl?"

"Darcy ... I meant talk to him, not bulldoze him," Vinnie muttered in my ear.

Maybe some of Maggie's anger had rubbed off on me. I stepped closer, getting into his personal space and to his credit, Tony didn't back away. Though his right hand gripped the edge of the bar until his knuckles went white. "Max doesn't have friends."

"Sure, he does. And I'm one of them. Now, be a decent chap and just tell me why you'd go after his family? I understand he owed you a lot of money. Surely you know it's not good business going around abducting innocent people."

Tony glanced over his shoulder and the sweat that had been making his cheeks shine dripped off his chin. I noticed dark patches under his armpits when he tried mopping his face with a cocktail napkin. "Look, as soon as he pays me what he owes, he'll get them back."

"You know, just because the sheriff in your town turned a blind eye to criminal acts, doesn't mean other people will do the same. What if Max went to the state police? Or even the FBI?"

"He doesn't have the gall for that. Besides, you think any of that would matter?"

"I don't know, Tony. You tell me."

He glanced over his shoulder again. I leaned out, trying to track what he was looking at. Clearly, something or someone was making the man even more jittery. Well, that didn't seem right for a man in charge of this sort of operation.

As I stood there watching the bookie continue to sweat profusely, a thought hit me. "You're not in charge of this, are you?"

All the cocktail napkins in the world wouldn't be enough to dry Tony's face as his whole body began to shake from what could have been terror or alcohol tremors. "Look, I didn't want to hurt anyone. Hell, it wasn't even me who took them. I didn't give the order. I just passed along a list of people who owed me big."

"Passed it to who?" I pressed.

"Just stop asking questions, okay? You don't want to wind up in trouble, too," Tony said, reaching for another shot glass.

Before I could ask him any further questions, a tall, well-dressed man with slicked back blond hair and a maroon tie that matched the servers' outfits descended on us. I noticed platform lifts in his shoes made him appear taller than he really was and the tailored suit clung to his thick frame like a glove. The green of his irises almost glowed demon-like in the ambient light as he looked down on me.

"What's going on here, Tony?" he asked in a

soothing baritone. Yet, there was almost an air of disinterest to his question like the answer didn't actually matter. It was just the appropriate thing to ask.

"Nothing. Just sharing a drink," Tony answered.

"Why don't you introduce me to your new lady friend?"

"Darcy," I said, extending my hand.

"Carl King and this is my establishment." He didn't bother to shake my hand. Instead, he gave me an appraising look, as if he were assessing a prize animal at auction or trying to figure out the price of a luxury car.

A shiver danced down my spine as I stood under his scrutinizing gaze. The way Tony shrunk into himself in Carl's presence told me all I needed to know. This man was dangerous, and I'd just put myself directly in his line of sight. *Bloody brilliant move, Darcy!*

9

I tried not to show my discomfort as Carl studied me with his intense gaze. Beside him, Tony continued to sweat. I could see the gears in the bookie's mind spinning, trying to figure out if he should throw me under the bus or pretend we actually knew each other.

"And who are you here with, Darcy?" Carl asked, gesturing to my wristband.

I glanced down, only now realizing that it was different from the one Maggie had been given. I could make out the words, 'Plus One' printed along the top. I swallowed the lump forming in my throat. If I admitted to being here with Maggie and not Max, that would make Tony suspicious. But if I said I was here with Max and they found Maggie instead, that could put her in danger.

"She's a friend of Max," Tony blurted, saving me from making the decision.

"I didn't think your boy Max had many friends." The sharpness in Carl's tone signaled he wasn't happy with Tony's statement.

"Actually, she's here with me." Maggie's voice came from directly behind Carl. My heart skipped several beats as the man turned to look her up and down. "And you are?"

"Max's sister, Maggie. He was understandably a little nervous with everything going on, so he asked me to come as his proxy."

I caught my girlfriend's eye and mouthed, 'What are you doing?' She just smiled and kept her focus on Carl. He tilted his head to one side as he stroked the smooth skin on his chin.

"That's not really allowed."

"Well, Max isn't the one who's been playing in the tournament, so he figured it wasn't appropriate for him to attend tonight."

"What the hell is she doing?" Vinnie asked in my ear, nearly making me jump.

"No idea," I answered as tight-lipped as I could manage.

"You know anything about this, Tony?"

Tony cowered beneath Carl's glare. "N-no. I swear."

"You look like the kind of person who knows what's really going on around here," Maggie challenged, stepping toe-to-toe with Carl. "You must know my brother doesn't play nearly as well as I do."

He reached out and cupped her cheek before leaning in close to stage whisper in her ear. "Sweetheart, I don't know you or your brother."

I shuddered as his hand stayed pressed against her face, giving her that same appraising once over he'd given me. I wanted to pry his fingers away, and defend the woman I loved. As I watched them square off, I could feel my magic bubbling to the surface, longing to be put to use. But I could sense no plants around us. Just concrete and old, unused spaces.

"Well, trust me, you want me in your tournament, and not him. I'm by far the superior player."

"We shall see about that." Carl finally peeled his fingers from Maggie's face. "I have a special in-person event happening here tomorrow. And I've got a game about to start for the tournament players to win entry. You last more than three hands and you're in."

"And why would I want to play in your game?"

"Because I hold all the cards, sweetheart. And if you win, you'll get anything you want."

The way he patronized her made my blood boil.

"Anything?"

"That's what I said."

"Fine. I'm in."

Carl pointed to a darkened corridor just past the end of the bar. "Go through there in twenty minutes. Don't be late."

With that, Carl slunk off, leaving Maggie, Tony, and I by the bar. I wanted to grab Maggie and shake some sense into her, to demand she rethink whatever insane idea she was concocting. But we couldn't let Tony in on our plans. Maggie's cheeks were flushed as she moved to stand beside me, her left hand finding my right.

"I'm going to get my family back, you arrogant prick," she snapped, staring Tony down.

"Look, I didn't know Max had family or friends, okay? He was just a customer who owed me big."

Wait, something he'd said rang like a bell in my head. "You said you gave Carl a list of people who owed you a lot of money. He took their loved ones, too, didn't he?"

"What do you think?" Tony reached for his now

empty shot glass. The bartender appeared, filling the glass to the brim. He looked a little glassy-eyed himself.

"Max said you used to be reasonable," Maggie spat.

"What do you want from me?" he whined.

"The truth would be nice," I answered, wishing Ginny was here. She'd pull it from his lips without even trying.

"I may have made a few bad bets myself, okay? I know I shouldn't mix business and pleasure, but sometimes I just couldn't help it. Usually, I make better choices."

"You owe Carl money, don't you?" Maggie said, her voice losing a bit of its edge.

"Look, I hope you can actually win here. I really do. But the rest of us, we aren't so lucky."

"He took someone you care about," I said, earning a small head nod in response. "Before or after they came for Max's family?"

"What does it matter? I am desperate."

"So, is Max. And I'm guessing the other people on your list are too. Why not report it to the police? We know about your connection with the sheriff in your town," Maggie retorted.

"You think he's stupid enough to go up against Carl King?"

I wanted to ask him more questions about the operation and who might have sent the message about magic being involved in all of this, but we didn't have time. We needed to figure out our next move.

So, I led Maggie away from the bar and back around the edge of the room. We slipped through the 'Staff Only' door into the empty, brightly lit corridor. At least now we'd have some space to talk without being overheard.

"Well, he's a piece of work," Maggie grumbled.

"Seems he's in the same position as Max," I noted. "Vinnie, Rick, did you hear any of that?"

"Yeah, we got all of it," Rick answered. "And Maggie, you have no business walking into that game. You don't have any idea who is in there or what the stakes are. It's dangerous."

"Doesn't matter. All I know is that my sister-in-law's life is on the line."

"Not just hers. There are other people, too. And ... I think they might be holding them here somewhere."

I reached into my clutch and retrieved the clue I

found earlier. "Oh, I found this pacifier in the kitchen back here."

"What pacifier?" Max's voice came through the comm link. Maggie snapped a photo and sent it to her brother.

"Oh, it looks like the ones we got for Aneesa." The fear in his voice was palpable.

"That means she could be close," Maggie said. "It has to be a good thing."

I made a sweeping gesture around us. "This place is enormous. We can't possibly search the whole complex."

"Maybe you don't have to," Vinnie replied. "What if you follow the staff and see where they get cleaned up? That might give us a hint."

"I don't know. The kitchen looked abandoned. The counters and everything were grimy and dusty, like it hadn't been used in ages."

"But the server you were with knew it existed."

"Server?" Maggie gave me a confused look.

I pointed to the top of my dress. "I had a bit of a champagne incident. One of the servers helped me get cleaned up. Honestly, it was a bit strange. She didn't seem to know how she knew where to go. She didn't even know if she was old enough to serve alcohol."

"Sort of detached like the woman handing out the wristbands," Maggie noted.

"Yeah. I mean, what if these people have been made to forget who they are?"

"Do you think that's what happens to the people Carl kidnaps?" Maggie sounded appalled.

"I don't get what the advantage would be of forcing them to forget who they are and who their loved ones are, if they expect people to clear their debts," I answered.

"We're going to need to do some digging into this Carl King," Rick said over the earpiece. "I'd really prefer the two of you get out of there."

"No. If Maggie has an in with Carl, she needs to keep following it. And like you said, I should follow up with the servers and see what I can find about this place." After a beat I addressed Max. "Max, did you ever hear Tony mention Carl before?"

"No. To be honest, I didn't even know he gambled, let alone ended up in debt himself."

"Okay, so Maggie's going to work on impressing Carl with her card shark skills and I'm going to see what I can find out around here," I said, trying to take charge of the situation.

"No, you should both get out of there. This man, he's dangerous like a predator," Rick said gruffly.

"We came this far. Besides, I doubt Carl would do anything to Maggie in a room full of witnesses. And I've got Beau to watch my back," I answered.

"Be careful. Both of you," Rick conceded.

I intended to be.

I planted a kiss on Maggie's lips and gave her hands a squeeze. "I'll meet you out front when the game is over."

"I just have to survive three hands. Can't be that hard," she said, her voice confident.

I didn't want her to jinx herself, but I stayed quiet. She smoothed the hem of her black dress, pivoted on her heel, and headed back to the main room. I waited, trying to decide if it was time to go invisible.

"What do you think mate? Ready to go incognito?" I addressed the reptile who'd been quietly clinging to my shoulder the whole time.

'Follow first.'

Beau had a point. People could have seen Maggie and I go in here together. If they didn't see me come back out, too, that would raise suspicions even more. I sucked in a breath and headed into the main space again. The crowd had thinned a bit, and I spotted a few people moving in the same direction as Maggie.

Surely, they wouldn't all be playing in the entry match.

The servers milled about, starting to pick up empty and discarded drink glasses. I spotted the young woman who'd shown me the kitchen earlier. She was hastily piling far too many glasses on her tray. No one seemed to notice or reprimanded her for poor technique. I resisted the urge to approach and tell her to take multiple trips. Instead, I simply watched the other servers working. They appeared to be young women and all of them shared the slightly glazed over expression when they looked up.

"Darcy, can you try and get some photos of the servers?" Vinnie's voice came over the comm link.

"Maybe? But why?"

"Just a hunch."

"I'll see what I can do. I'll try to get some of the guys. The bartender looks like he's got the same expression as the rest of them."

Okay, time to go invisible.

"Alright, Beau. Let's see where they go."

Still hiding in the shadows of the empty alcove where no one could see me Beau let his magic rip. My body shivered as the reptile's magic danced down my spine, cool sensations followed by warm until I couldn't see my own hand in front of my face.

Thankfully, the area was carpeted as I hurried forward to fall in line with the servers. The bartender stepped out from behind the bar and another man waved everyone towards the 'Employee Only' door.

"Back inside," he called.

The women hurried out of sight, as did the bartender, and I did my best to keep up with the group. As soon as we passed through the door, I regretted not removing my heels to avoid any unnecessary noise as we traveled across the tile flooring. But none of them noticed an extra set of footsteps trailing them. They marched two by two down the corridor, past the kitchen, and into another room.

My heart stopped the moment I realized what I was seeing upon entry. Small groups of people—mainly women and children—sat huddled together around the room. I picked out Chloe in the far back, trying to shush a whimpering baby. My fingers itched to return the dropped pacifier.

I retrieved my phone and tried to take as many photos of the servers and the other women and children in the room as I could. Before I had a chance to send them to Rick, a strange sound echoed through the space and something on the walls was growing brighter.

*'Get out'*

Beau's words were barely audible in my mind as the sound intensified, setting my teeth on edge. My stomach made an uncomfortable, nausea-inducing flip.

Somehow, I managed to back out of the room just as the light popped like a flare and the room went silent. I picked up on the sound of bodies hitting a hard surface and pushed the door open again. Everyone now lay slumped on the floor, unconscious.

"I found Chloe and a lot more people. But they're all unconscious," I whispered, knowing Rick and Vinnie would pick up my words.

"Where are you?" Rick sounded all business.

"Somewhere past the kitchen, I think. It's within the same corridor at least. Just straight back through the 'Employee Only' entrance. Something happened that knocked them all out."

"You need to get out of there now!" Rick ordered. "We'll take it from here."

I was about to follow his directive when I noticed something slender and green poking out from one of the server's pockets. I stooped down and plucked it free. Somehow, the girl had managed to get a bit of grass stuck in her uniform. The tiny shoot quivered in my hand. It must have been transferred recently enough to still hold some life within it.

"Darcy, I want to see you walking out those front doors in a minute," Rick insisted.

"Just give me one second."

Still invisible, I loosely held the grass in my palm and allowed my magic to trickle into it, making it a vibrant green. It grew in length, and I wound it around the server's wrist like a bracelet. I mimed tying a knot and the strands knit together, securing itself around her hand.

"I need you to come with me. Just a piece of you so I can follow it back to her," I whispered to the grass strand.

It quivered again, though more hesitant this time before it extended its length and allowed me to gently pluck part of it free.

I stored it in my clutch and eased the door shut. I hated the idea of leaving them alone in that room, especially not knowing what was in store for the captives next. But Rick's insistence that I get out was enough to make me backtrack until I made it to the main room again. It stood vacant now. So, I hurried through the doors, passed the young woman who'd given us our wristbands, and burst into the night air.

Beau dropped his magic camouflage when we'd

cleared the building and Maggie's car came into view. Max appeared from behind another parked car and bowled me over before I could reach the passenger side.

"You saw them? Are they okay?"

"Get in the car," I hissed, shoving the man inside Maggie's car before anyone could see him. I rounded the front of her car and climbed into the front passenger seat.

"They looked okay. But they are unconscious at the moment ... all of them."

"Let me see the photos," Vinnie requested through my comm link.

I texted the deputy the images I'd taken and turned back to watch the front doors, holding my breath. Would Maggie be joining us again soon? It couldn't possibly take that long to play three hands of poker. As we stood waiting, I had the uneasy thought of what would happen if she failed to make it into the VIP event.

*Come on, Maggie. Please hurry back to me.*

**10**

The wait for Maggie felt interminable. Every time the door opened, my head perked up and my shoulders fell once I confirmed the person walking out wasn't my girlfriend. I resisted the urge to text her, not wanting to interrupt her concentration during the game. The two lawmen had stayed in their parked car. I assumed busying themselves with Vinnie's hunch. I wondered what it was since he still hadn't bothered to share anything with me. Max stayed low in the back seat, glancing from me to the front door and back again.

"You're thinking about going in," I said, interrupting his brooding.

"How'd you..." he trailed off.

Beau materialized on my shoulder and tilted his

head to one side. I patted the creature's scaly back. "I could say a little chameleon told me, but it's pretty obvious that you want to bust in there and find your family."

"I don't understand why your police friends aren't busting down the doors right now. You saw people being held against their will. Shouldn't that be enough probable cause or whatever to go in?"

"I'm not a lawyer or a police officer. Most days I don't even come close to pretending I know anything about the law. But one person claiming they saw a bunch of people who looked scared probably isn't enough. Besides, Carl gives off some uncomfortable vibes. I mean, Tony's cousin, the sheriff is afraid of him. That alone should tell you something."

"Yeah, Tony is a scheming prick."

"He might actually be in the same position as you right now," I said softly. "Whether before or after your family was taken, it sounds like kidnapping debtors families is Carl's motive of operation ... and it doesn't matter if you work for him or not. If you get on his bad side, or you owe the wrong person money, that's how he collects."

"Doesn't make me hate Tony any less."

Just then, the front door of the secret event opened, and Maggie stepped out into the midnight gloom. I climbed from the passenger seat and ran forward, flinging myself into her arms. "I was starting to think you weren't ever coming out."

"I'm okay," she said, giving me a firm hug. "I'll fill you in when we get away from here. Something tells me we've got eyes on us."

I couldn't help but look around for any sign we were being watched. Nothing stood out. However, if Carl was as slick as he appeared to be at first glance, I wouldn't find any evidence we were being surveilled. Max continued to stay out of view in the back seat of Maggie's car before Maggie and I slid into the front seats.

"We should meet somewhere back in Brookhaven to debrief," Maggie said to the empty air around us. It took me a moment to realize she was speaking to Rick and Vinnie through her comm link.

"Ginny's," Rick answered.

The café felt awfully public for the conversation we were about to have with everyone. Though it also meant that if we were being followed, it wouldn't lead right back to the police station or the B&B. Hopefully, it would keep Tania a little safer for a bit longer. The ride back to Brookhaven was otherwise quiet. Even the sense of anxiety gripping my chest eased slightly as the familiar tree line off the highway just beyond the town's borders came into view.

*'Will rescue them.'*

Beau's voice was soft and reassuring in the back of my mind. I hadn't even realized I'd been thinking about the captives in that room. I stroked the reptile's scales on the very top of his head absently as Maggie found a parking spot outside Ginny's on Main Street. The lights were still on, and I spotted Ginny standing by the front door. She turned the lock and opened the door as we approached. The bell overhead rang out a second time when Rick and Vinnie walked in. The deputy carried a small tablet I hadn't seen him using before, his brow creased in concentration.

Ginny made a gesture for us to take any table, and she headed for the kitchen, presumably on the hunt for fresh coffee. We were going to need the caffeine boost given the late hour.

Rick slid into a booth and Vinnie settled in right beside him. Max squeezed onto the end of the bench seat, giving Maggie and I more space opposite them. Ginny returned with mugs and a full pot of coffee before leaving us to our business. Vinnie laid the tablet on the table between us, sliding his finger across the screen rapid fire.

"So, did you get into tomorrow's in-person tournament?" I addressed Maggie.

"Barely, but yes, I've secured a seat."

"I can't believe he actually said if you won the whole thing, you'd get anything you wanted," I added, failing to hide the disgust in my tone.

"I can't say why exactly, but I got the feeling it wasn't just money at stake," Maggie noted. "A couple of the other players said they'd heard that the markers for the game are tied to, uh ... physical lots."

"That's disgusting," Max spat.

"So, how are we going to get back in there and rescue all those people they're holding?" I eyed Rick and Vinnie for answers.

"We're already getting things ready to go back tonight," Rick answered. "The photos you took should be enough to get us in front of a sympathetic judge. Especially since we've identified Max's wife and that ties directly into the case we're investigating."

"You'll still have to be awfully convincing if you're granted an audience at this hour," Maggie said through a yawn.

"Screw the judge. Let's just go back and get them now," Max protested, slamming his fist on the table.

"We aren't going to just go busting down doors

like vigilantes, because I also did a little digging on Carl King. He's been at the center of some racketeering investigations. Nothing strong enough to stick, but he's on the radar of some pretty powerful people."

"He's slick. I wouldn't be surprised if he's got law enforcement in his pocket, too," I noted. "I mean, Tony didn't seem like the brightest bulb. I'd imagine he had to learn how to extort the law from somewhere or just copied a bigger criminal."

"Probably TV," Max grumbled.

"I might have a theory on why the wait staff at the event looked the way they did. Or at least why they were used," Vinnie started, turning the tablet to face Maggie and me. He flicked through a couple of the photos I'd managed to take after everyone passed out. "There are a handful of missing person reports dating back at least a year. Some of these women look as if they match those reports."

"But why would Carl risk trotting them out now?"

"My guess is because the people who were looking for them have given up. Or they weren't invited purposely to this little gathering," Rick replied. "He's keeping these people as collateral for a reason. We need to find out why."

"If you're able to rescue them, do you think that

would be enough to arrest Carl?" I watched as Vinnie continued flicking through the photos, until he stopped on one that matched the young woman who'd shown me the kitchen.

"It certainly wouldn't hurt the case. Especially if Chloe is able to identify the men who took her."

"Could what Ginny and I saw at the flat help with that?"

"As much as we appreciate your magical talents, I don't think a regular court is ready to accept them," Rick answered. "Now, I know Maggie needs to go back there tomorrow for this tournament, but you three must stay away from the premises until then. Got it?"

"Wouldn't dream of going back there without you," I said.

Vinnie let out a snort. "There was a time I would have believed that. Like five cases ago, maybe."

"Oi, I behave." Mostly.

"We won't go near the place," Maggie affirmed. "If anything, I need to spend some time brushing up on my poker skills with real cards. I've always been more of an online player."

"I can help with that," Max offered. "I may not be great at gambling, but I can at least deal cards."

"I don't know much about the rules, but I'll help any way I can," I offered.

Ginny reappeared, carrying five plates of cheese steaks, setting them in front of us. "I'm guessing none of you have had an actual meal tonight."

"Might as well grab a couple to-go boxes. We need to head out," Rick answered.

"We'll eat here," Maggie noted.

Ginny retreated to the counter and plucked two boxes from just out of view. In quick succession, she'd transferred the sandwiches to the boxes.

Max slid out of the booth to allow Vinnie and Rick to exit. Before the deputy scooped up the tablet, I took note of the missing person file opened showing a young woman's name, Katie Stewart. They might be off plotting a rescue attempt, but I wanted to know more about the girl who helped me. Something had been off about our interaction, and I didn't think it was entirely related to the other missing person cases.

As Rick and Vinnie turned to leave, I caught a familiar glint in Rick's eyes. The normally brown irises had picked up a strong amber sheen. He didn't need to say a word to convey that he had all this under control. And just maybe, if things went sideways, he'd unleash his inner wildcat to take Carl down.

I definitely did not want to be around to witness that sort of potential carnage.

Max settled back in the booth across from Maggie and I, staring at the menu still sitting there. He picked at the edge of the lamination and Maggie reached across the table, grabbing his hand with her own. "We're going to bring your family home. One way or another. And we're going to clear your debt with Tony while we're at it."

"I want to believe you, Magpie. But my wife needs me more than ever and I'm just sitting here eating a damn sandwich."

"You're taking care of yourself. I'm sure she'd want you to do that so you're in a good place to help take care of her and your baby when they're home. Because they are going to need you," Maggie retorted. "We will all be here for them when that happens."

Despite insisting he felt guilty about sitting and eating, Max devoured his sandwich before I'd even gotten through a quarter of mine. Outside, street-lights hummed, casting small pools of light across the darkened sidewalk.

"I found a bit of grass on one of the servers

earlier. I managed to get it to grow, and I've got a bit of it with me. If anything happens, we can probably use it to see through the plant."

"See through the plant?" Confusion colored Max's tone.

"Oh ... uh, I can sort of see things from a plant's perspective when I've built a connection with it. It's been really helpful in solving some weird mysteries that happened around town."

"She's being modest. She used it to track people across islands," Maggie said proudly.

"And it's how I was able to see what happened to Chloe at your flat. She had a flower in the kitchen, and I was able to use my magic to sort of access its memory."

"What are we waiting for then?"

"Because we promised Rick and Vinnie, we'd stay out of it," I answered. "It's just a last resort sort of thing."

"Are you serious? You've got power and you're just too scared to use it."

His tone was biting, but I couldn't blame him. He was scared and frustrated and to him, it looked as if we were doing nothing to remedy the situation.

"That isn't fair," Maggie interjected.

"No, really, it's fine. He's right. Come on, why

don't we go back to Tania's, and I'll see what I can? Besides, maybe Rick and Vinnie could use the information."

Maggie tossed a couple of bills on the table, and we left the cafe behind. In a matter of minutes, we'd reached the B&B and found ourselves settled in the living room. I held the tiny offshoot of grass in my palm. It had dulled a bit since being separated from the original blade, but it perked up when I nudged it with my magic.

"Let's just make sure everyone is where we left them," I whispered to the grass, and it began to vibrate against my skin. Unlike when I'd done this at the carnival grounds, I didn't take Maggie along for the ride this time. A moment later, my vision went green, and the living room fell away. When I blinked, the space that surrounded me was unfamiliar. The woman whose wrist I'd affixed the grass bracelet to was in a completely different position and I couldn't see Chloe or the others anymore. What was going on?

**11**

"arcy, what do you see?" Maggie's voice sounded miles off.

"Things have changed," I answered. "I think maybe the girl's been moved?"

"Where is Chloe?" Max's voice joined the conversation.

"I've no idea. All I saw back there was that one room and the kitchen."

I felt a hand on my wrist, Maggie's familiar grip. "Just describe what you see now."

I swallowed and tried to focus on what the blade of grass showed me. The woman had been lying down when I'd slipped the makeshift tracking bracelet onto her wrist. She now appeared to be upright, her back pressed against something solid, like a wall. It was difficult to make out any colors and textures from the plant's point of view. Everything just had that same greenish gauzy look. But the people I could see from my vantage point appeared to be the other servers, including Katie. She looked the most alert of the bunch oddly enough. I watched as she moved around the room, checking on the others, pressing her fingers lightly to their pulse points on their necks and wrists.

"The woman who bumped into me, Katie, she's checking everyone to make sure they're okay."

"Maybe she was just the first to come to," Maggie suggested.

"What about the others you saw? Where's Chloe and Aneesa?" Max sounded desperate.

"I, uh, don't know. I don't see them."

"What else can you make out about the room? Furniture? Size of the space?" Maggie attempted to guide me.

I pulled my focus away from Katie to take in the room. Tall shelves lined one side of the room. They were barren, but they didn't appear as grimy as the unused kitchen. Someone had used the space recently enough to clean it. The opposite wall was bare, but I thought I could make out something like hooks protruding high up on the wall.

"The space looks like maybe a utility closet of some sort," I answered. "Perhaps twelve feet deep? Or a little more? I don't know exactly, but not very big. The people are pretty well crammed in, two across on the floor."

"Okay, that helps," Maggie said.

I willfully severed my connection to the blade of grass and sat back, blinking until the living room returned. "I honestly don't know what happened to the others," I said, eyeing Max apologetically.

"Maybe Rick and Vinnie will find them," Maggie suggested. "In the meantime, I want to find out everything we can about Carl."

"What about practicing your poker skills?" I reminded her. "You need to be as good as possible to stay in the game. Did Carl say he would be playing in the game?"

"He didn't. But I heard rumblings from the dealer that he might jump in for the final round."

"Maggie and I can practice," Max said. "Why don't you look up Carl?"

Maggie fixed her brother with an annoyed glare. She clearly didn't appreciate him volunteering me for research duty, but I didn't mind. I grabbed Maggie's computer and settled it on my lap as I watched them pull one of the end tables between the couch and chair. "Let me see if Tania has a deck of cards." Maggie left the room and Max rubbed at the nape of his neck.

I did my best to focus on the task at hand. A quick online search of Carl King brought up the fact that he owned a few casinos in the Midwest. Interesting, I hadn't picked up any accent or twang in his voice. But just because he owned property out there didn't mean he was originally from the area. Seeing he had assets out west suggested he might have some here in Massachusetts, too. Finding those records took a little more digging. After a solid ten minutes of searching—Maggie had finally returned with a slightly torn deck of cards—I found that he owned what used to be a strip mall. It had been abandoned the last five years. There were notices of stalled construction on the premises. He'd considered converting it into another casino, but the permits had fallen through or been stalled. Apparently, he didn't have his hands in all the right pockets to get his deals done easily.

"Find anything useful?" Max dealt out five cards each to himself and Maggie.

"Just that I'm pretty sure we were at the property he owns here in the state. It used to be a strip mall that went belly up about five years back. It's sat vacant ever since." I watched as Maggie studied her cards, picked two from her hand and laid them face down on the table between them. "A strip mall would actually make sense. We were probably either in what used to be the food court or a restaurant. And the closet or maybe a changing area, I saw could have been in any store?"

Max picked up Maggie's two discarded cards and dealt her new ones. She studied them, rearranging what was in her hand. "Uh, isn't there meant to be betting or something going on right now?" I prompted.

Maggie waved me off. "That part I'm fine with. It's just the actual card holding and having a good poker face. Not exactly something you need when you're playing against a computer screen."

"Fair enough."

I turned my focus back to the computer in my lap. I tried to find anything else I could on Carl, but nothing obvious came up. Of course, there wouldn't be records of any ongoing investigations, especially if they hadn't resulted in him being brought in for questioning. But I did wonder about his private life. Did he have people in his life who knew what he was doing? I tried searching marriage records in the state, but nothing came up. Except all that meant was he hadn't gotten married here in Massachusetts. I clicked back to the real estate listings from the Midwest and randomly picked Kansas followed by Minnesota where he had property. The Minnesota marriage records popped up with documentation for a Carl King to a Lilian Stewart.

"Stewart?" I murmured under my breath.

Maggie and Max were too engrossed in their game to pay me any mind. It showed the couple had been wed twenty-two years ago. I didn't see any record of a divorce and no evidence they'd had any children in the state. But it couldn't be a coincidence that Katie shared Lilian's last name. I wish I'd thought to take a photo of the missing person's photo Vinnie had found on Katie.

With a little luck, it wasn't just a police record. Maybe Katie's family had put up missing posters online somewhere I could track? Putting the search terms 'Katie Stewart missing' brought up a single news article and a couple of posts on a Facebook group. The posts were all made by someone named Lili Stewart. Lilian possibly?

"I don't mean to interrupt ... but I think I might have found the young woman who I ran into, Katie."

Maggie laid her cards down. "What did you find?"

"Well, a marriage record for Carl in Minnesota to a woman named Lilian Stewart. Katie's last name is Stewart, too. I also found a missing person's post on a Facebook group from a Lili Stewart referencing Katie."

I turned the computer, so Maggie could see the screen and opened up the posts. I could only see a brief summary of the post as I wasn't a member of the group. It looked as if her first post in the Missing Loved Ones group went up six months ago. Her daughter, Katie, had gone for a visit with family and vanished. She'd been unable to reach her daughter since and although police spoke with the family's relatives, there were no leads. A second post from about two months ago showed a plea from Lilian to Katie, begging her to come home.

"You think Carl is her father?" Max piped up.

"Maybe. I mean, I hope he's not so depraved to mess with his own daughter's memories. But I mean that message Maggie got had to come from someone who knew what was going on. Who better than his own daughter?"

"But even if that's true and she's with him voluntarily, why reach out to me of all people?"

"I hate to break it to you, Sis, but the fact that magic is openly accepted here in Brookhaven isn't really a secret out there in the world. People know what goes on here. And for all we know they were tracking your IP address and pinged you here in town."

"Maybe she's trying to stop whatever her father is up to?" I suggested. "I mean I saw her checking on everyone else. She was fully alert while everyone else wasn't. Either she's the one knocking them out, or she's trained herself to resist it."

"Or she could be a plant to keep them compliant," Maggie said. "It wouldn't be the first time we've seen a parent and child teaming up to use magic to harm people."

"That wasn't the vibe I got," I insisted. "Nothing like Elise and her mum."

If anything, it felt more like Walter in his search for his sister. A relative seeking to rescue and protect, rather than harm. I clung to the hope that Katie was on the right side of this mess. I couldn't stomach the alternative, not when so many other lives were in peril.

"Could we message her back on the tournament site? Maybe we can convince her we want to help and come up with a plan together?"

"But what if it's totally unrelated?" Max proposed.

"I mean the online gambling platform isn't at all like an in-person event."

"Except the event invitation came through it, and I got the impression Carl is open to using any means necessary to conduct his business," I countered.

With Maggie's computer still in my lap, I navigated back to the tournament site and found the messages from earlier in the day. My fingers shook a little as I started to type.

**You were brave, letting me know that people were in danger of forgetting who they are. It must have been scary for you to break that silence.**

I waited as the screen remained blank. I wanted to dip back into my connection with the grass and see if Katie had access to a computer to respond. It would at least give me confirmation that she had been on the other end of the messages. But even as I tried to reach out to the offshoot blade of grass with my power, it shrunk back, as if I'd exhausted its reserves already.

"Come on, Katie. Answer back," I pleaded under my breath, my gaze never leaving the screen.

I tuned out the sound of Max shuffling the deck and the cards hitting the table as he dealt another hand. I blocked the sensation of Beau dislodging himself from my shoulder and moving to settle on the couch beside me. All of my focus zeroed in on the computer screen, praying for her reply. It felt like eons, but was likely only a couple of minutes until one came.

**It's not bravery when it's behind a screen.**

I hurriedly typed a response back.

**You made the first step of reaching out for help. You are saving lives. I want to help you and break the spell. Tell me what I can do?**

Her answer came faster this time.

**Not safe here. Too many eyes.**

I sent another response.

**I can find you. At the game tomorrow.**

The screen went blank again for what felt like ages.

How will I know it's you?

Part of me understood she was expecting to find Maggie or even a bloke on the other end of this correspondence. So, I needed to give her a way to find me.

I'll have a red rose in my hair.

Another pause and then her reply.

After the game starts.

It was the beginning of a plan, at least. I didn't know what exactly she wanted to tell me, or how we'd break the spell over the other players' abducted family members. But it was worth taking the risk to find out.

"I think I'm meeting Katie tomorrow once the game begins."

"Well then she obviously knows you aren't me," Maggie said. "She'd have to know I'm playing in the game tomorrow."

Before I could respond, Maggie's phone buzzed with an incoming video call from Vinnie. Max and I crammed in around her to see the screen as she accepted the call.

"Please give me some good news," she said.

"Afraid it's bad news. We got the warrant to search the premises. We went in the same way you did, followed Darcy's directions to the 'Staff Only' door. But there were no closets or anything off the hallway."

"What about the kitchen?" I asked.

"Nothing. It's just a giant empty hall that dead ends near what appeared to be an old loading dock. But there's no evidence that the doors had been opened in years. The place is massive. Maybe we mixed up the entry."

"Or they're using magic to conceal what they're hiding. I was able to see the server I magically tagged."

"You did what?" Rick's angry face came into frame. Even on the screen the flash of amber in his eyes as his temper flared was unmistakable.

"When I found them all in that room, one of the servers had a blade of grass on them. I managed to use it to track their location. The servers looked to have been separated from everyone else. And we might have an inside man ... err, woman. Possibly

Carl's daughter, Katie. She's been marked as missing for the last six months."

"I remember seeing a Katie Stewart in the files I pulled up," Vinnie noted. "Didn't see anything linking her to King though."

"Honestly I haven't either, but I mean she's got the same last name as his wife and reports say she was off visiting family when she disappeared."

"Well, we're going to keep looking and see if we can come up with anything else. You stay put at Tania's until the morning. Maggie, you don't head to that game without police backup."

I tried not to let the worry build in my chest—constricting my lungs and making it hard to breathe. Maggie and Max needed me to be strong. After all, if things with Katie fell through, we still needed Maggie to bring the house down.

*S*leep eluded me. I found myself sitting in the darkened kitchen at four in the morning nursing my second cup of coffee. Even though my body ached, and I kept failing to stifle yawns, I knew I had little chance of going to bed. I'd have to tough it out for the rest of the day. After all, we were close to getting to the bottom of Carl's unsavory business and rescuing Chloe and the others. At least that's what I kept telling myself.

"You look like crap," Sam noted nonchalantly as he floated through the wall opposite me. He stopped at the other chair and cast a sad look at the furniture before continuing to bob in midair.

"Every time I close my eyes, I see Katie's face and I just wake up."

"This is a weird one for sure," he said, his tone turning serious.

"I don't think anything we've dealt with has been this dangerous," I admitted.

"Well, I mean there was that vampire on Haven Island. And the killer carnival folk."

"But they weren't exploiting people like this. Not in the same way. To make someone forget who they are? It's barbaric. You just erase someone's identity and for what? Money?"

"I have long been of the opinion that people are ... what's the British word I'm looking for? Hmm ... Wankers."

"Not everyone," I reminded him.

"Enough that they have whole industries dedicated to tracking them down and locking them away for their depravity."

"I suppose you're right. I just feel a bit off kilter I suppose. Sure, I've been in situations that have targeted people I care about before, but this just feels worse somehow."

"Well, you're going to be the hero and save the day like always. Because that's just what you do."

"I appreciate your confidence in me. But honestly, I'm not feeling it right now."

"You just need more coffee," he teased with a smirk. "You know Tania has some of Ginny's extra potent blend in the back of the cabinet over the sink. The stuff apparently works like jet fuel."

More coffee on an empty stomach wasn't a bright idea. So, I set my empty mug aside and rummaged in the fridge for some eggs. Scrambling them in a pan, I set about making some toast and sausage to go along with it. I found some strawberry preserves in the cabinet and slathered it on the toast before going in search of Ginny's special jet fuel blend.

By the time I'd settled in at the table, the stove clock read 5:10. At least it was a more respectable time for people to be awake. I heard footsteps just beyond the kitchen and my head perked up when I saw Tania come into view. She arched a brow at the pans I'd left sitting on the counter and the half-full pot of coffee.

"Someone's been busy."

"Couldn't sleep," I answered around a bite of scrambled egg. "I'll clean up, don't worry."

"I know you will. And I could feel your anxiety all the way upstairs."

"Sorry."

"Hazard of being an empath, remember?

Honestly, it helped block out Max's sorrow and Maggie's nerves."

"We're all just one big emotional mess," I said. "The sooner we take Carl down and get Chloe and the baby back, the better."

"I know you want to be the hero, but you don't have to be, you know. That's why Rick and Vinnie are involved. They're trained to take those risks."

"Don't rob her of her savior status," Sam teased.

"Hush."

"I know I don't need to ... I'm not proving anything to Maggie. But maybe I feel like I need to show Max that I can be there for him and his family."

"Why do you think that is?" Tania sat down next to me at the table.

"Because I love Maggie, and I want to make a good impression on her family. I want to be in her life for as long as possible and if she's mending her relationship with him, then that means I'll be in his life, too. I want him to know he can count on me."

"You see him as your family, too?"

"Maybe one day, if I'm lucky."

"Well, *por favor*, be careful. I think we all know that Maggie wouldn't want you taking any unnecessary risks on her account."

"I will."

"Good, now eat your food before it gets cold." She stood and approached the coffee pot, pouring herself a cup. She took a sniff. "I see Sam told you where I keep Ginny's special blend."

"I'm going to need all the caffeine I can get."

She raised her mug in a cheers gesture and took a long swig. "I think we all will."

The food wasn't anywhere close to Tania's cooking standards, but it did the trick. With a full belly, I headed upstairs to get dressed in as comfortable clothes as I could manage while still looking professional. Even if I was snooping around Carl's makeshift casino, I needed to show that I belonged. I found Maggie sitting on the bed staring at her hands.

"You, okay?" My words caught her off guard and her blue eyes looked up in surprise.

"Sorry, just thinking."

"I've been up half the night, so I'm there with you." I sat beside her on the mattress. "Want to share the burden?"

"I just keep circling back to why Carl took all of those people and why he's wiping their memories. I mean, I can sort of understand using them as leverage to collect on debts. You get people to keep gambling to win back their loved ones. But assuming people actually manage to get the money together, what then? Does he just return them? I feel like there's got to be more to the story. And the more I think about it, the more I'm terrified for Chloe and Aneesa and all the other people you saw in that room."

"I have to believe that Katie is going to help us crack this wide open. She's the connection to Carl that I'm sure he's not counting on anyone finding. Maybe he took his daughter to keep her quiet and she's fighting back now. Or maybe she purposely infiltrated his organization. Either way, I am going to get answers. Rick and Vinnie can use that information to bring Carl and his operation down for good."

"And then I worry about you snooping around under Carl's nose. There's still so much we don't know about the man. Clearly, he has power and he's not afraid to use it. And if Tony's cousin in law enforcement is scared of him ... "

"I'm not powerless. I know I look like a mild-mannered gardener, but I've got skills, remember? I have your back and Max's too."

"I just don't want to ruin it all by losing." Tears sparkled unshed in her eyes, and I couldn't help but pull her into a protective, bear hug.

"You are going to do amazing. No matter how the game turns out, you are going to do great. We will find a way to get Max out of his debt. I mean, I'm pretty sure with Tony going to jail for his part in all of this, his debt might even be erased."

Maggie let out a sharp laugh. "I'm not sure my brother has that kind of luck. Besides, like you said, it sounds like Tony is a victim, too."

"Whatever happens, your family is going to be okay. I'm going to make sure of it."

"I love you," Maggie proclaimed and gave me a kiss.

"I love you, too. Now come on, you need to get ready to wipe the floor with this prat."

I left her to change and after grabbing my own clothes, I made my way to the bathroom for a quick shower. The water washed away the lack of sleep—that or the coffee was starting to hit my system—because I felt energized when I stepped out a few minutes later. By the time I made it back downstairs, I found Tania had cleaned the pans I'd used and was making breakfast for the rest of the house.

"You look a little better," Tania noted with a smile when she saw me.

"Guess Ginny's coffee really did the trick."

Just then, a knock came at the front door. I pivoted

and made my way to the front door. Opening it I found Vinnie and Rick standing on the front steps.

"Morning." I took a step back to allow them entry. "Tania's made breakfast."

"Thanks." Vinnie looked as exhausted as he had while working on the carnival case. Clearly, sleep had eluded him, too.

Rick just look determined. He marched past me and headed into the kitchen. "Everything okay?" I asked Vinnie in a low tone.

"Other than the fact we searched that place all night and found nothing? Sure, everything's great."

"There has to be magic at play," I suggested. "I mean I know what I saw. I couldn't have been hallucinating it."

"You weren't. I was finally able to pick up on the scent of bodies, but I couldn't track it," Rick answered as Vinnie and I walked into the kitchen.

"You aren't a bloodhound," Tania noted. "Your senses, even enhanced, aren't meant for that sort of thing."

"I don't like magic getting in the way of my investigation," Rick snapped. "People who have that sort of power and who use it to hurt people deserve worse than prison."

"He's just been in a mood all night," Vinnie explained, trying to brush off his boss' overly aggressive statement.

"Here, food and coffee will help." Tania physically steered Brookhaven's Chief of Police to the table on the far side of the kitchen and shoved him into a chair before placing a plate of food and coffee in front of him. "Eat."

To his credit, Rick sat in silence, picked up his fork, and started eating.

"I'm assuming we'll have communication devices again. That way you can track us and know what's happening."

"That's the only way I'm even considering letting you two go back in. If I didn't think it would put you in more danger, I'd suggest body cameras," Rick answered in between bites of eggs and steak. "But earpieces will have to be enough. We'll be recording everything that comes through the comms just like last time."

"You expect Carl to confess while he's playing poker?" Maggie appeared in the entryway from the dining room.

"I doubt we'll get that lucky," Vinnie answered.

"So, what exactly is the plan going in?" I settled

across from Rick. "Does Carl know you raided the place last night?"

"Oh, I'm sure he did. That's probably how he was able to hide everything from us. I wouldn't be surprised if he sent out different instructions on where to go for the big game today."

"Hang on, he doesn't have a license to run a casino here, right?"

Rick cocked his head to one side. "He does not." A pause and then he added, "... We could hold him for operating an illegal gambling operation. Use the time to search the place in the light of day."

"But what about all the other people coming to the event? Surely, they think they are going to play to win their loved ones' freedom?" Tania suggested.

"We'd sweep everyone up and sort out the liability issues after," Rick replied. "It's not a bad idea though."

"Wouldn't it be better to catch him running the game? Arrest him when he's actually playing?"

"Most likely."

"That won't happen until the final hand," I reminded them.

"Then it's going to be up to Maggie to get him talking, keep him occupied until we can bring in some help to take him down," Rick answered. "But the minute things get dicey, you two are going to get the hell out of there. No big dramatic shows of power. We give the signal, and you get out."

His words stung a little, but they carried truth in them. I couldn't promise I wouldn't try to do everything I could, magical or otherwise, to bring Carl down. "We will stay out of your way."

"Vinnie will be on Maggie's comms," Rick said, fixing me with an intense look. "I'll be with you."

The better to keep an eye on me I imagine. Some things never changed.

Still, I couldn't say I was upset to have the lawman watching over me. I knew he'd jump in if things got too hairy. "So now we just have to get there and hope all hell doesn't break loose."

Maggie's p glanced down at her laptop screen and then back to the two men in the room. "Looks like the location is the same. There's no mention of the place being raided by the police at all. Either he thinks we're all stupid or he knows you found nothing and assumes his dirty secrets are safe."

"Either way we know where we're headed," I replied.

"I think until everything is resolved, your brother needs to stay here at the B&B," Vinnie said, addressing Maggie.

"I will keep Max occupied. After all, we will need to have things prepared for when you bring his wife and baby home," Tania said calmly.

"I'm surprised he's not awake and climbing the walls with anxiety," I said, looking around the kitchen.

"I may have given him some extra strong chamomile tea last night," Maggie admitted with a sheepish look. "At least one of us needed to get a good night's sleep."

Maggie's phone buzzed again. "Apparently, we aren't allowed a plus one this time around."

Bollocks, that threw a bit of a spanner in the works. But only a minor one. "Simple, I'll tag along, bring Beau, and slip in unnoticed."

"Don't forget your rose," Maggie reminded me and tapped the side of her head.

Rick and Vinnie exchanged confused looks.

"I told Katie that she'd recognize me by the rose in my hair."

"Flower up then. We need to get going if we want everything set up before the game starts in a few hours."

I left the kitchen and moved into the dining room where a beautiful arrangement of roses sat on the small table by the window, soaking up the sun. I plucked a red bloom and secured it in my hair before going in search of my reptilian friend. Beau lounged on the arm of the couch.

"Hate to ruin your nap, mate, but I need your help again. We've got innocent people to rescue."

**13**

My heart hammered as Maggie's car approached the abandoned strip mall as the clock in the dash ticked over to 9:05. I sat hunched down in the back seat, doing my best to stay out of sight. The tournament was set to start at 9:30 according to the message she received. We had arrived with just enough time to get her inside. I scanned the lot, trying to find Rick's car, but I didn't see it. Well, that was probably the point. If they were running proper surveillance, they shouldn't be seen. They'd already made sure we each had our earpieces.

"Should we go over the plan one more time?" Maggie sounded nervous. She smoothed the dark blue off=the=shoulder silk dress she'd chosen for the occasion and I couldn't help but admire how tightly it hugged all of her curves, even in the drvier seat.

"You keep playing as long as you can. Try to last until the end and get Carl talking. I'll find Katie and help Rick get the victims out. See if I can put the pieces together on what Carl planned to do with everyone if I can."

"I never wanted us to end up in this sort of situation."

"No one does. But we're getting out of this mess. Because of you, we have a real chance of rescuing a lot of missing people. Just focus on that."

"I still can't help feeling responsible."

"Don't go there, Maggie. You had a struggle that you overcame. You are strong. Just because you had this one thing in your past doesn't make you responsible for anyone else's actions, not even your brother Max. You are a healer, but you're not meant to heal the whole world's problems."

"Imposter syndrome is a bitch."

"You have nothing to feel like an imposter for. You're the real bloody deal Maggie Henley. And don't let any of those wankers in that game tell you otherwise."

"Thanks, I think I needed that."

She reached for the handle on the driver side door, but I stopped her. "Give me your phone."

"What for?"

I made a grabbing gesture, and she handed it back to me. I tossed it on the floor beside me. "We need an excuse for the passenger side door to open, just in case anyone's watching."

"You are brilliant."

"I have my moments."

As Maggie climbed out of the car and secured her earpiece, I slotted my own device in my right ear. Beau positioned himself across both of my shoulders, resting his front claws lightly on my left collarbone. His magic rippled over me just as Maggie rounded the back of the car, looked down as she approached, and then opened the passenger side door. She stepped back just enough to let me get out before she reached in and grabbed her phone.

"See you on the other side," I called as she walked off.

Part of me wanted to stick close for as long as I could, to follow her inside and walk her to the door of the game room. But it was safer if we weren't together just in case whatever spells they had running inside interfered with Beau's invisibility. So, I scanned the lot until another car pulled in. An older gentleman in a wrinkled brown suit climbed out of the driver seat. I hurried to fall in step behind him and held my breath as he opened the door. I slipped inside and watched as the same woman from the day before checked him in, gave him a wristband, and took his phone. They hadn't taken phones last time. I spotted Maggie's in the bin, too. Carl wasn't taking any chances of being spied on after last night.

After a moment of hesitation, the man in front of me handed over his phone and pulled open the interior door. Somehow, I managed to squeeze through before it shut on me. The interior was brighter than it had been the day before and with the extra light I could make out bland grey carpeting on the floor that led down a short corridor. Two large men—the same ones I'd seen come to take Chloe and the baby from the apartment—stood guard at the end of the hall. The man I was following approached, held up his wrist, and one of them opened the door to allow him entry. In the brief moment the door was open, I saw three or four different tables set up, all with dealers shuffling cards and practicing laying them out. It appeared Carl had set things up so that people had to last multiple games to make it to his table at the end.

"You've got this, Maggie," I whispered under my breath.

"You need to go find Katie," Rick's voice said through my earpiece.

"I'm on it," I said under my breath and turned to figure out where the staff might be. The space in front of me was completely empty. The bar and all of the tables had been removed. The 'Employee Only' door remained. I hurried toward it and paused. Realistically, I should wait for someone to come through so I could follow them, but time wasn't exactly on our side. I didn't see any servers walking around to give me cover. Having to take the chance, I pushed the door inward, stepping into the corridor beyond. I heard voices coming from somewhere down the hall and to the right. Creeping along as quietly as possible, I made my way in that direction until I found the entrance to the kitchen. The center islands had been shoved all to one side and a group of people sat crammed together in behind them, as if they were being barricaded inside. I hadn't done a proper headcount the day before but this looked like it accounted for the servers and the other hostages I'd seen. Shiny metal handcuffs secured them to the legs of the islands. I spotted Katie at the far end of the room.

"It's going to be okay," she told an older woman with a short gray bob and a visible bruise on her cheek. "I have to go now."

Katie hurried from the room, wiping tears from her cheeks as she did so. I hurried after her, trying to decide the best time to drop Beau's invisibility. She'd nearly reached the door back into the main space.

"Wait," I called.

My voice rang out in the confined space and Katie spun on her heel. Beau, sensing the situation, dropped his concealment over me, while still keeping his own presence hidden. Her eyes widened as she took in my sudden appearance out of thin air. Her lips moved wordlessly, and her finger pointed to the red rose in my hair.

"I knew you had to be someone with magic," she said. "I just knew it."

"You're Katie Stewart," I said, taking a step closer. "You knew who you were yesterday when I asked. Why pretend you didn't?"

"Not here."

She grabbed my wrist and hauled me back down the corridor, turning left several times until we ended up in what looked to be an old office. It was just as dusty and neglected as the kitchen had been. Katie wore the same outfit I'd seen her in the day before. In fact, I could smell the remnants of alcohol on the fabric.

"How do you know who I am?"

"I may have taken a photo yesterday and compared it to missing persons records. Your mum is really worried about you."

"She'll manage."

"You're his daughter, aren't you? Carl King. The man running this whole operation."

"Only by marriage. My real dad died when I was a baby. Freak car accident, so my mom claimed. Though, given Carl's ... uh, love of control, I wouldn't put it past him to have orchestrated it, just so he could marry my mom."

"I'm sorry to hear that ..." After a moment, I continued, "You reached out, wanted someone to know what was happening. Why not go to the police?"

"Do you know anything about that man? He's untouchable."

"I know he's operating this poker game illegally. He doesn't have a license to run a casino or anything like it," I answered. "I also know that law enforcement agencies have been trying to bring him down for racketeering."

"You have a friend in law enforcement or

something?"

"A couple actually. And they're waiting to bring him down. Please, help us do that." I took a step closer to the young woman. "I believe that's why you're here with me now, and why you reached out ... You want all of this to stop."

"Of course, I want this all to stop. I mean, he's a horrible man. I've hated him for years. He took all of my mother's money and just skipped town."

"Who did she think you were visiting before she filed the missing person's report six months ago?"

"I've got an aunt on her side out this way. I stayed with her for about a week while I went looking for Carl. When I found him here in Massachusetts, I took off. I didn't tell my aunt where I was going, just in case he was watching her."

I gestured to her uniform. "The other people who were acting as servers yesterday, they're all people he's kidnapped, aren't they?"

"People with family who never paid their debts. Or the ones that no one else wanted."

"Wanted?"

"You didn't think he just kept them around for fun, did you?" She shivered, the movement making her shake from head to toe. "He holds these elite games and the people who make it to the end, they get their pick."

My stomach performed a flip, and my breakfast threatened to make a repeat appearance. "You mean he's selling people?"

"Say that again Darcy? It sounded like you said he was selling people," Rick's voice came through my comm link.

"He keeps people gambling, giving him all their winnings in the hopes of freeing their loved ones, the same people he's magicked to forget who they are or that they're even missing. And the unlucky ones, the poor souls get sold off to the highest bidders."

I tried to keep the bile from rising, but the reality of Carl's depravity struck me way too hard. I cast about, finding a grimy rubbish bin under a table and grabbed it, emptying my stomach's contents in short order.

"Talk to me, Darcy," Rick ordered, his voice insistent in my ear.

I let the dry heaves subside before answering. "Sorry, that's just ... how has no one found out before now?"

Katie tapped her temple. "Anyone who gets too close just forgets."

"Ask her how she's managed to evade detection."

I swatted at my ear, forgetting for the moment that Katie didn't know I had a communication device listening. "If he's your stepfather, surely he'd recognize your name, even if he hadn't seen you in ages. You did say you feared he was watching your mum's family."

"When you blend in with the people he doesn't care about, it's easy to go unnoticed. Besides, I lied and gave him a fake name. I made up a whole profile online that was terrible at gambling, so that I'd end up in debt and he'd send his thugs to come get me."

"That's pretty ballsy."

She shrugged. "I wanted to get everything I could to take him down."

"What does he do with the people he's taken and mindwiped?"

"He knocks them out and transports them in big catering vans. They don't stay in one place for too long. I heard him talking about heading back out to the Midwest soon. I don't know, maybe things are too hot up here with all the permits falling through."

"Then we need to stop him before he can leave town." I turned my back to her and addressed Rick. "What should I do now?"

"Who are you talking to?" Katie's tone got sharper, edged with fear.

"Try to find any documentation of these sales, see if any money's changed hands for human beings. Anything we can use to take him down," Rick answered.

"I told you I have friends in law enforcement just waiting to bust in."

"You're a cop?"

"Lord no. I care for plants at a marijuana dispensary and I'm a witch. Carl hurt people I care about. So, I'm going to do everything I can to bring him to justice." I pointed at her outfit. "People in uniforms tend to get overlooked right?"

"Yeah. So?"

"So, I am starting to come up with the outline of a plan. I need to find whatever logbooks he's got showing all of his dealings. Maybe I could do that if I'm in uniform."

"What was the point of Beau then?" Rick muttered.

"To turn invisible, but it puts strain on my friend who is lending me his magic. I don't want to hurt him." I tapped my ear, so Katie didn't think I was talking to thin air. "I've got police on comm link.

Anyway, Katie, do you know where Carl keeps the books?"

*Please say somewhere in the building.*

"The server room back past where everyone's playing."

"Katie, first I'll need you to show me."

She produced a pen and a cocktail napkin, and sketched out a rough map. "We're here. You need to go straight through the main hall we were in last night, through the door here." She drew an x on another spot, labeling it the 'Game Room.' "Then once you're inside, there's going to be two doors side by side. One's the server room. The other they're using for storage."

I reached up and dislodged Beau from my shoulders, forcing him to momentarily become visible. "Katie, take Beau with you. He's how I turned invisible before. He can extend his magic to you and a couple of other people. Get the other captives out of here. Beau should be able to shield a few of you at a time."

"Send them out the west exit. We've got EMS standing by," Rick said.

"Take them to the west exit. Help will be waiting."

"And what about you?"

"I'll be fine." I pointed to her uniform and then to my outfit. "Time for a wardrobe change."

In a matter of minutes, we'd exchanged clothes, and Katie led me back the way we'd come. "The server room is through one of the two doors at the rear of the game room."

"Any suggestions on what excuse I could give to get back there?"

"Well, they moved the bar into the room, too. They might be storing extra vodka and rum in there."

"Got it."

As I made my way back down the corridor, I felt a rose petal as it fell from my hair, landing on the floor. I bent to pick it up so as not to leave evidence behind when a little shock jumped from the petal to my hand. My magic bubbled to the surface, and I understood what the plant intended. It was leaving me with a bit of floral power to tap into just in case I needed it.

"Thank you."

I heard voices in the kitchen grow louder as Katie explained how they were going to get out. It wasn't fair to put all of those lives on someone so young, but she'd risked her own safety to uncover her stepfather's nefarious enterprise. She seemed more than up to the task.

"No unnecessary risks in there," Rick's voice sounded in my ear as I approached the corridor leading to the game room.

"Understood."

As I reached the door, still manned by Chloe's kidnappers, I felt another petal subtly flutter to the floor. Neither man noticed and the one on the right pulled the door open without a word. The atmosphere within the room was tense. Two of the four tables I'd seen earlier were now empty and only a handful of players were left around one table. It didn't seem as if enough time had passed to get through that many hands and whittle the players down that much. Yet, the clock on the wall read nearly 10:50. Could Carl manipulate the time, too?

"Focus, Darcy," I chided myself and spotted two doors next to one another. Everyone's attention was on the players at the far table. No one even blinked when I slipped through the door on the right, finding a room full of whirring servers and a small laptop perched on a low table.

14

Oh, how I wished Maggie was with me. She was far better with computers. As I stood in the room, looking around like a complete moron, I caught a glimpse of my girlfriend at the table. At least she was still in the game, playing for the win. I eased the door shut behind me, so I wouldn't be disturbed.

"How's she been doing?" I addressed Rick.

"Focus on what you're doing."

"Please, just tell me. It will help put my mind at ease."

"She's been holding her own. Placing really big bets that have paid off. Cleared the tables pretty fast."

"That was her doing?"

"Mostly. Not the strategy I would have gone with. Doesn't afford us a lot of time to get people out."

Maybe she was trying to get other players out of the line of fire, so she could spend time with Carl one-on-one.

I opened the laptop on the table to find a locked screen. *Bugger*. Tapping the space bar brought up a login window with a prefilled username, but no password. Looking the machine over, I noticed a slender black drive plugged into one of the USB ports on the laptop.

"Uh, I don't know what to do now," I confessed in a strangled whisper. "I'm not a hacker. And there's no way I could even attempt to get in before the system kicked me out for too many wrong password attempts." I could have used Maggie's magic hacking skills to whip up a program to get the data. But she was too busy trying to keep Carl distracted.

"We can worry about decrypting it later."

"But you need evidence to arrest him," I protested. "There's some sort of external drive attached to the laptop."

"We've got the people he's been holding coming out. That's enough to let us come in and arrest him. Just take the drive and get out of there."

Oh, how I wished I hadn't given Beau to Katie to

help her get the kidnapped people out unnoticed. He could have helped me sneak the drive out of the room. But maybe I could find another way. I'd gotten into the room unnoticed. Maybe I could get into the makeshift supply room for the alcohol without anyone catching on, too.

I closed the laptop and left it where I'd found it. I pressed myself against the wall and listened to the noises coming from the room outside. I heard the subtle flicking of cards being dealt, and low voices contemplating their next bets. I nudged the door open and found everyone still focused on the game. I reached out my left hand and groped for the door to the supply room. It opened and I flung myself out of the server room entrance—leaving it ajar—and into the next room.

A handful of bottles were sitting on a crate, but I didn't see anything resembling a case or anything I could sneak the drive out inside. Until my gaze landed on a stack of serving trays. If I balanced things just right, I could slide the drive in between some of the trays and take it out of the room. It was worth a try anyway. And if all else failed, I'd just shove the bloody device down my top. My heart hammered against my ribs as I grabbed as many trays as I could find.

I held them in front of my torso like a shield and hurried back to the server room and the waiting laptop. I unplugged the external drive, offering up a silent prayer that I hadn't just corrupted all of its data and stuck it between two serving trays at the bottom of the pile. It looked a little odd, but I could still probably conceal it if anyone stopped me. Time to get this evidence to Rick and Vinnie.

I made it out of the server room and shut the door behind me when one of the guards who'd been watching the game room entrance spotted me. He crossed the distance in a matter of moments and towered over me, his right hand resting on the grip of his gun at his hip.

"What are you doing?"

"I ... I'm sorry," I stammered, trying to imitate a glazed over look. "I had to get trays."

He waved his hands around at the people in the room. "You see anyone asking for drinks. Get back with the others before I do something you'll regret."

"O-okay."

I hurried past him and out into the main room. I could feel his gaze on my back as I crossed to the 'Employee Only' door. I made it through and heaved a sigh when I knew the brute could no longer see me. The corridor was quiet, and I moved with fast steps to the kitchen. It was empty. Katie had done it. She'd actually gotten everyone out.

"Did you get anything useful?"

Katie's voice behind me made me jump and the top few trays fell from my hands, clattering onto the floor.

"I don't know his password, but I got his drive. Can you get it to the police?"

"He won't have much on there, believe me I've looked."

"You said he keeps ledgers. You told me to look in the server room." I gripped the remaining trays and the external drive tighter to my chest as I turned to face the young woman.

"You won't find everything you want on there is what I meant." She made a grabbing gesture for the drive. "I'll take it out to them."

I took a step back. "Maybe I should hold onto it after all?"

"I'm not like him. I don't hurt people. Please, I swear on my mother's life I will get it right to the police." She pointed at my ear. "You still have them in your ear, right?"

"You there, Rick?"

"I'm here. Vinnie, too."

"Did she bring the missing people out like we asked?"

"Yeah, she did."

"Chloe and the baby, are they okay?"

"A bit confused and exhausted, but yes."

*'Can trust her.'*

Beau's words echoed in my mind like a soothing balm. My lizard friend had never steered me wrong before. He always had my back and been a good judge of character. I still hesitated for a moment before handing over the drive to Katie.

"You don't happen to know how to access the drive, do you?"

"He was always too careful, never accessing it even with people he had mindwiped around. No matter what he did they could always remember something he didn't want them to know."

"So, if he doesn't keep the accounting on his computer, where does he keep it?"

"A paper ledger he has with him at all times."

I didn't recall seeing anything like that on his person yesterday during our brief interaction. But maybe that was the point. It was too brief of an interaction, and it had been dark. Also, I had been a little off kilter, not expecting to meet him in the first place.

"Okay, I'll see if I can get that from him."

"No, you need to get out here now," Rick ordered.

I took the communication device out and handed it to Katie along with the external drive. "I'm not leaving Maggie in there with the villain."

I could pick up crackling from the device as Rick no doubt protested my decision to abandon the only link I had to him and backup. But I wasn't going to let Maggie get hurt. Besides, I had my own defenses that Carl didn't know about. With any luck, he wouldn't see me *coming*.

*'Need extra stealth.'*

I held my arm out towards Katie and Beau rippled into existence before crawling off her shoulder. He nestled against my collarbone like always and I relished his familiar weight. Time to go save my girl.

Katie held the drive close to her chest and looked at me, unshed tears suddenly sparkling in her eyes. "Thank you for helping stop this monster."

"It's what we do," I said before thinking better of it.

We parted company in the corridor. I waited just long enough for her footsteps to dissipate before I retraced my steps through the open space and back towards the door to the game. Only one of the guards was present now, but that still posed a problem. They'd sent me off to join the other waiters. They weren't expecting me back. And I doubted I could convince the man to just let me in.

I stopped a short distance away to consider my options. This was the only one way in and I wasn't about to leave Maggie behind. But I wasn't physically capable of taking this brute of a man down. Not without a lot of help.

*'Use the power at your disposal.'*

"How?" I asked through barely parted lips.

The rose still tangled in my hair, somehow dislodged it's petals and floated down to settle on the back of my right hand. That same jolt I'd gotten from the flower before zipped through my body again, reminding me that I had plant life in this place I could tap into. And the fact the rose had come from my home, somewhere I'd been able to nurture it and bond with it, made our connection that much stronger. I heard it in the back of my mind, practically begging me to put it to good use.

"Just let me think," I whispered to the petals. I took a step forward to get a better sense of the man opposite me. He wasn't nearly as beefy as the one who'd kicked me out of the room, but he could still inflict some serious damage if he wanted. Just like his colleague, he was armed. The gun should be my first priority. Grappling with a man twice my size was one thing, but doing it with a weapon in play was downright suicidal.

Slowly, a picture took form in my mind's eye. I saw thick vines with sharp thorns wrapping around the weapon, dislodging it from its holster, and tossing it as far from the man as possible. Then dozens of wild roses would erupt from the vines, encircling him, and dragging him to the floor in silence.

In theory it should work. But that assumed I could make it happen almost simultaneously and keep the man quiet. Of that I had little confidence. I'd have to settle with just taking him out of the equation. I pressed my back to the wall running perpendicular to the doorway he guarded and poked my head out just enough to make sure he hadn't moved.

"Let's see what we can do here."

Power prickled along my skin as I plucked a petal from the back of my hand and cupped it in my palm. I envisioned the thick vines with thorns growing from the petal, changing its form just enough to be what I needed. It turned almost liquid, shifting in color through the rainbow like an oil slick before it grew solid again in my hand, changing itself to thick and green and weighty. A small patch was on the rough exterior, devoid of thorns and it wrapped loosely around my hands before extending to the floor undulating in a snakelike slither. It wound its way along the ground, keeping to the shadows as I urged it onward. The moment it was within striking range, the end of the vine split in two, branching off into a V shape, one side wrapping around and up each meaty thigh. The left one grew larger with sharp thorns that dug into the fabric of his pants.

The man let out a surprised grunt of pain and surprise. Luckily, it didn't draw the attention of anyone inside the room. He reached down, trying to free himself from the plant creeping up, using his body like a trellis. The vines were relentless as I fed them more power, guiding them. The one on his right leg angled itself to free the weapon from its holster, sending it skittering away out of reach.

Time for the roses. I plucked the final petal from my hair and waved my free hand over it, encouraging it to bloom anew. It grew large and fragrant in my fingers and as the heady scent of roses filled the corridor in front of me, I realized the vines had taken their cue and gone into overdrive.

"Let's stay out of sight as much as we can," I told

Beau and felt his magic ripple over me from head to toe.

The vine remained wrapped around my unseen hand in midair as I hurried down the corridor. The guard still struggled against his floral restraints and as he opened his mouth to yell out, I stuffed the bloom I'd created into his mouth. With a firm yank of my right hand, the vine retracted, dragging him down the corridor out of my way.

The door remained closed, but I knew he hadn't needed a key to unlock it before. I could just open it and walk in. The room beyond had gone quiet as I reached for the handle. That should have been my first warning that something was wrong. Yet I carried on, charging in as if I owned the place.

The scene in front of me looked almost like a tableau frozen in time. Two other players were seated at the table, their hands in mid-motion as they were putting down their cards. Maggie's back was to me, and I couldn't see what she was doing with her hands. Carl was at the table, too, taking up the dealer's position.

The other guard was nowhere to be seen and that worried me. I realized too late that discarding my earpiece left me unaware of what Vinnie and Maggie had communicated as a plan to get Carl to talk and reveal the location of his ledger. Bloody hell, I'd truly gone and mucked this one up, hadn't I?

Muffled sounds came from the corridor behind me, and I turned to see the guard still struggling to free himself. The roses continued to pop out from the vines turning him into a giant man-shaped rose-bush. Beau's claws dug into my shoulder in warning, but it was too late for that, too.

That same sound I'd heard the day before when all of his victims had fallen unconscious filled my ears and the lights grew brighter. Panic gripped my chest as I tensed for the sudden loss of awareness, but it didn't come. Instead, Beau's magic vanished, exposing me to the man on the other side of the card table.

"Darcy, isn't it? Why don't you join us?" Carl's voice was icy and calm, as my mouth went dry, real-izing he had a gun trained on Maggie's chest.

15

The other two players sitting on either side of Maggie slowly set their cards down and tried to back away from the table. Carl clucked his tongue at them, and they stopped moving. Keeping the gun trained on her, he used his free hand to indicate a chair at one of the other tables. Swallowing my fear and the bravado I'd had coming into the room, I pulled a chair over, squeezing in beside Maggie.

"You know, the invitation this morning was very clear. No plus ones. I'm disappointed you didn't follow directions sweetheart," Carl chided, his tone unchanged, glaring at Maggie.

"It wasn't her fault," I blurted.

The gun swiveled to point in my direction, and I froze. "It isn't polite to speak out of turn."

"I didn't know she followed me," Maggie said, keeping her hands flat on the table. Four playing cards sat in between her hands, as if I'd interrupted them mid-game.

"Well, I'm not sure I believe that."

"She's telling the truth. She told me it was just her allowed today. But I didn't want her to be alone, so I followed," I lied.

"And your outfit, you just happened to come dressed as wait staff?" Carl sniffed the air. "You certainly smell like them."

"I knew I needed a way in, so I found one," I replied. "You wouldn't miss one of your servers. It isn't like they're working today."

Maggie glanced at me, real fear in her eyes. I could see her forearms trembling as she exerted as much control as she could not to ball her hands into fists or try reaching for my hand. This conversation wasn't getting us anywhere except putting the other players in more danger. I didn't fancy Maggie and I being alone with this man. But at least if it were just us, the collateral damage could be minimized.

"Look, I clearly interrupted your game, and I really didn't mean to do that. Please, I'll sit quietly like a good girl and let you all finish. To be honest, I've not had a chance to see the pros at work."

I hoped a little flattery might ease his nerves and get him to lower the gun.

"Is that so?"

"I'm rubbish at cards," I admitted.

"Then I suppose it's a good thing you aren't playing," he sneered. He leaned back in his chair with the gun still pointing my way and tapped his chin with the index finger on his free hand. "Alright. You can watch. But I think we're going to need to up the stakes a little."

"What do you mean?" Maggie's voice carried a small quiver in it.

"Well, I am a man of my word. If you win, you get anything you want. If I win ... I get your friend here."

"Oh, hell no!" Maggie roared, jumping to her feet.

Carl's gun moved to focus on her again. I reached out and grabbed Maggie's wrist, pulling her back into her chair. "It's fine. Really, just accept his terms."

"I am not gambling your freedom away to this barbarian," Maggie shouted.

I leaned in as close as I dared. "All of the victims are safe with Rick and Vinnie."

"I know," she whispered back.

I caught Carl watching us and I kissed her cheek. "I believe in you. Just accept his terms."

"Fine."

Carl smirked at us and laid the gun across his lap, still within easy reach. I didn't hear the guard sputtering and fighting for his freedom in the corridor any more, which only mildly surprised me. Carl's magic-busting wards or whatever he had in place had definitely disrupted my connection to the spell, but that was the least of our worries right now.

"Let's place your bets ladies and gentlemen," Carl declared, collecting the cards everyone had been playing with. He shuffled them as the players on either side of us considered their options. I couldn't ask them to stay, but I also wasn't confident what would happen if they left.

Carl dealt the cards far faster than I'd seen Max do the night before during practice. I wasn't even sure everyone ended up with the proper number of cards until they picked up their hand. I looked at Maggie's cards over her shoulder. She had a nine, ten, and Jack of Hearts in her hand, along with a Queen of Diamonds and a two of Clubs. I longed to ask her what her strategy was, but I kept quiet.

The man on the far left pushed two fifty-dollar chips forward. Maggie did the same, as did the man to my right. Carl considered the markers on the table and smirked. "Raise two hundred." He slid two fifty-dollar chips forward plus another pair of one hundred-dollar chips.

I eyed the man on the far left. He shook his head. "I'm out."

I studied the markers in front of Maggie. She had enough to match Carl's bet and then some. She'd clearly been winning more than the others. After a moment, Maggie slid two one hundred-dollar chips forward, saying, "I call."

"Too rich for me," the man on my right said with a sigh, laying his cards down.

"Looks like the bet's back to me," Carl said with a cheshire grin. In an overexaggerated motion, he shoved all of his markers into the center of the table. "All in. No need to drag out the inevitable."

The guard I'd lost track of appeared from the supply room and grabbed each man by the bicep, hauling them off their feet. They both started protesting, but with a simple wave of the gun from Carl, they fell silent. I watched as the guard shoved them both in the room he'd just exited, and slammed the door shut. He shoved a padlock onto the handle and secured it in place.

"Go help our other friend out there," Carl ordered.

Without a word, the man disappeared, leaving us alone in the room with Carl. I watched Maggie as she studied her cards again before carefully setting them down. For a split second I feared she was about to back out of the game. She shoved her considerable pile of markers into the middle of the table. "I call. All in."

Carl turned his attention to his own cards for a moment. Maggie picked hers up again and plucked out the Queen and the two, laying them face down in front of her and pushing them in Carl's direction. I hated being the damsel in need of saving. "Why do you do it?"

Carl's head snapped up. "Do what?"

"Barter with people's lives? I can understand wanting to collect on debts people owe you, but kidnapping their loved ones just makes people desperate. And desperate people make mistakes. They don't win big."

"You've got a mouth on you, don't you?"

"Consider it my British curiosity. Come on, if you're about to own me, don't I deserve to know what I'm in for?"

"Don't have as much trust in your friend than you let on, hmm?"

"Not like I'll remember it," I said, hedging my bets.

"I don't need these people's money. I make plenty from my casinos out west. This ... this I do for fun."

"You're buying and selling human beings. It's obscene!" Maggie snapped.

"Please, people are obscene sometimes," he answered with a shrug.

"You just like to use people, because it makes you feel powerful. And you think just because you've got magic on your side, that you won't get caught."

"Well, it's hard to get caught when no one knows they should ask for help."

"You didn't count on them remembering who they were. Well, I've got news for you, Carl. You've got a flaw in your house of cards and it's about to topple all down."

"I don't know what you're talking about. But don't worry, it won't matter soon. Because you're right, you won't remember anything in a few short minutes. And then, if I do have a rat, I'll hunt them down."

He moved Maggie's discarded cards out of the

way and dealt her two new cards, the seven and eight of hearts. Maggie had ended up with a straight flush. I didn't know a lot about poker, but I knew enough that it was a strong hand. I looked around the room as Carl selected one card for his own hand. There had to be a way I could disable the magical wards in here.

"Time to see if your friend is as good as she's claimed to be," Carl announced. He set the gun on the table beside him, just out of my reach.

"Put your cards down first," Maggie said.

Carl clucked his tongue at her. "That's not how this works. Ladies first." His hand moved to rest on the handle of the gun—an added threat.

"I hope you have a plan if this goes south," Maggie said just barely loud enough for me to hear her. I couldn't tell if she was talking to me or to Vinnie in her ear. Either way I wouldn't be able to hear his response or give her an answer myself.

My palms grew sweaty as I watched Maggie arrange her cards and lay them down on the table. "I think I'm pretty good."

Carl let out a laugh. "Oh, you are good. Maybe I'll keep you both around just for the entertainment value. But you should know to never bet against the house." He turned his cards over one at a time, laying out an Ace, King, Queen, and Jack of Clubs.

He still held one card in his hand, no doubt pausing for dramatic affect.

*'Cheating.'*

Somehow, even though Beau's magic had failed to keep me hidden after I came back into the room, it hadn't disrupted his ability to blend in. It was only then that I realized he'd somehow moved from my shoulder and was now near my leg. Where a tiny piece of rose petal sat waiting. I lowered my right hand towards the floor, letting my magic bubble to the surface, just enough to make a connection with the flower on the carpet, but hopefully not enough to set off Carl's warning system.

"You know what, before we end this game, I just have to know who gave you that uniform?" Carl's words cut through my concentration and the power sputtered.

"I don't owe you any answers," I replied. His features darkened and he reached for the gun again, as if it was the only thing he could use to intimidate me.

"That's not the answer you want to give. Not to me."

"Do you talk to the people you supposedly care about like that? If you do, it's no wonder you're all alone. No friends, and no family to speak of."

Carl's lips curled. Bugger, did I just give Katie away? "I knew that little bitch looked familiar. And I should have realized that little message that went out across the whole platform came from her."

"What message?" I feigned ignorance.

"Don't play with me. I know she sent out a message to every player with that cryptic warning about forgetting who they were."

Katie hadn't known Maggie—or Max—were magical from the start? She'd just sent it out to everyone, hoping someone would respond? That was definitely a risky move on her part. And if Carl knew about it, why had he let it slide?

"You aren't going to hurt her any more than you already have," I declared, my own anger over-whelming my better judgement.

"That's not for you to decide," he replied all smug, and laid down a Ten of Spades on the table. "In fact, you won't be deciding anything ever again. As I'm sure your friend can attest, my cards beat hers."

"Darcy ... I ... " Maggie trailed off, horror written all over her face.

I wasn't ready to give up yet. I rose to my feet and held my hands out in front of me. I could feel the rose petal on the floor, itching to be molded by my power and I let it run wild. It's thorns and stalk rose up through the table, cracking the wood with an earsplitting noise, sending playing cards and markers toppling to the floor. It wound its way to the gun first, wrapping so tight around the metallic surface I half-expected a shot to ring out. Instead, the thorns encased it entirely, so that the gun was just swallowed up.

"I don't belong to anyone," I proclaimed just as I heard the rhythmic tromp of multiple footsteps coming down the corridor. The calvary was finally on its way. I waved my hand towards Carl as he reached for something in his suit jacket's pocket. One of the vines I controlled beat him to it and inside I found a tiny device with a trigger. I guided it over to Maggie.

"Check his other pockets. I think he probably just cheated to beat you."

Maggie carefully picked her way around the writhing vines and roses that began popping up everywhere. She patted the man down, finding another card—a seven of Clubs—tucked into his sleeve. She held it up to his face and made a clucking sound of her own.

"I would think someone who runs a casino

knows the bad rap people get for cheating the house."

The roses began to cover his tailored suit. They wound around his wrists in makeshift handcuffs just as Rick burst inside, his own gun leveled at the man. "Sorry we're late. Had to deal with some weeds to get inside."

"We're fine," I replied, taking Maggie by the hand. "In case you missed it, he admitted to engaging in human trafficking for the fun of it."

"Oh, we got it all," Rick answered as he moved to bear down on Carl. He roughly patted the man down, tugging something small and rectangular from an inner jacket pocket. He flipped through the book and held it up for Maggie and me to see. "This should be everything else we need to put him away for a very long time."

"No, you have nothing," Carl howled as he fought to free himself from the vines. He only succeeded in tearing large holes in what must have been expensive fabric. I eased up on my magic, letting Rick take him into custody properly. As he and Vinnie led the man away, I caught sight of Katie in the distance. She mouthed, 'Thank you' at me before she followed additional uniformed officers from the scene.

For the first time in days, I didn't wake up exhausted by the worry that had gripped me. Maggie's family was safe, as were the rest of the kidnapped spouses and children we'd rescued. The B&B was quiet, but there was a serenity about the place that wiped away any lingering hints of unease. The other side of my bed was empty, and I sat up, looking around the room. I spotted a pile of dirty clothes at the foot of the bed and the closet door sat ajar.

My phone said it was only 6:30. Still, I couldn't go back to sleep, and it appeared Maggie was already up. After a brief trip to the bathroom, I padded down the stairs and heard a soft, melodic voice coming from the kitchen. I closed the distance and found my girlfriend rocking baby Aneesa in her arms, a bottle in one hand.

"You look like a natural," I commented quietly, so as not to disturb them.

"Thanks." The infant grabbed at the bottle and Maggie artfully positioned it in the baby's mouth. Contented sucking sounds followed.

"Where's Chloe and Max?"

"Given everything they've just been through, I thought they could use the rest. Besides, I've only just met my niece. I'm making up for lost time."

Despite the trauma the child had just endured, Aneesa appeared perfectly happy in her aunt's arms, nestling comfortably against Maggie's chest. She knew she was safe in Maggie's embrace. I leaned on the edge of the counter beside my girlfriend, peering down at the sleepy infant.

"Did you have any idea all of this would have come from your brother turning up on Tania's doorstep unannounced?"

"God, no!" Maggie set the partially drunk bottle on the counter and repositioned Aneesa to burp her. After a few gentle pats on her back, the little girl let out an impressive belch. "But I have to admit, I'm glad Max took a chance and showed up here. There were so many more people hurting than we could have known. And Carl would have continued to hurt even more people if we hadn't gotten involved."

"I know." Silence fell over the kitchen as Maggie repositioned the baby, offering up the bottle again. Aneesa sleepily batted it away with one tiny hand. "I won't lie, seeing you get so invested was scary."

"I didn't mean to worry you. I knew I couldn't go too deep, because I had you there, reminding me of the life I have now ... the life I can't afford to throw away if I really got sucked back in." Maggie began walking around the kitchen, rocking the baby until her eyelids drooped, and she slept soundly in her aunt's embrace. "I know it's not entirely fair to put that responsibility on you."

"It's over now and we're all okay. You got your family back. And we did a good thing. We saved lives. That's all we can ask for."

"Have I told you how much I love that stubborn streak in you? The one that insists on fighting for justice when someone is wronged?"

"I didn't do much, at least not this time around. You were the one in danger. But I'll always take risks when the people I love are in jeopardy. You all mean too much to me to lose."

"Thank you." Maggie slowly moved from the kitchen, through the dining room, and into the living room where a small travel crib sat by the couch. Maggie laid the baby down. Aneesa gave a soft whimper before quieting again. Maggie watched the baby for a moment longer before failing to stifle a yawn.

"I'm tired, but I know I won't be able to go back to sleep."

I reached for her hand. "Come on, I'll make us some coffee, because there's no way I can go back to bed either."

We retreated to the kitchen, and I started the coffee percolating. It bubbled and rumbled softly in the background. I caught Maggie glancing towards the living room every few minutes.

"We're close by. If the baby starts to fuss, it won't take long to get to her," I said, squeezing Maggie's hand.

"I know, I just ... I never thought I'd love someone so instantly. But she's got my heart wrapped in her little fists and she's not letting go."

I let out a little laugh. "I know how that feels. It's exactly how I felt when we first met, even if I wasn't quite ready to put it into words to anyone."

EARLY MORNING TURNED into late morning, and the rest of the B&B's guests made appearances. After sleeping in, Max looked far less pale and waxy, and Chloe's dark circles under her eyes had faded. A shower had helped, too. Tania came down around 9:00 and started making breakfast. Remarkably, Aneesa slept until thirty minutes later before waking up for another feeding.

"A guy could get used to this," Max proclaimed when he sat down at the dining room table, pulling the platter of Belgian waffles his way.

"You are fully capable of making breakfast," Chloe chided him with a small smile. "But it is very kind of you to do all of this for us."

"You are family," Tania replied. "And you've been through a terrible ordeal. You deserve some pampering and care. That is what we do for the people we care about here in Brookhaven."

Chloe looked around the table. "Maybe we should move here?"

Max let out a snort. "Maggie loves me, but I don't think she wants to share an entire town with me. Not again."

"Distance does make the heart grow fonder," Maggie teased and swiped a waffle from her brother's plate with a wink.

He gave her an eyeroll before dousing his breakfast in a healthy serving of syrup and fresh strawberries. "Don't worry Magpie, you can have your space. But I also promise not to be a stranger."

"I can live with that. Besides, I'm going to need lots and lots of visits with that beautiful little girl out there."

"She's taken to you very quickly," Chloe admitted, giving Maggie a grateful smile. "That's not something we've seen before."

"Yeah, even when mom and dad come by, she's usually screaming her head off," Max added.

"Happy to help. Besides, I've always liked babies."

"I think she recognizes your healing presence," I said.

"Darcy is right. I can sense that the baby is much calmer when Maggie is around," Tania added from the head of the table.

A companionable silence fell over the table, and I busied myself with breakfast. It felt so normal, just sharing a meal with family around the table. For a brief moment, a pang of sadness invaded my happiness. I would have loved to share this moment with members of my own family. There would be time to remedy that someday, I reminded myself.

Across the table, Chloe reached for the coffee

pot, tipping it over her mug to find it empty. I was on my feet, reaching for it in a matter of seconds. "Let me take care of that."

"Thanks."

I hurried into the kitchen to make a fresh pot. Just as I hit the button on the coffee maker, a sharp knock sounded. "I'll get it!" I called. Closing the distance from the kitchen to the front door, I nearly walked through Sam's translucent form.

"Could give a girl some warning," I chided and sidestepped the ghost.

"Rick's outside," Sam announced, ignoring my comment.

I fixed him with a surprised expression. "No cheeky nickname for him today?"

"Would it make you feel better if I called him Chief Kitty?"

I snorted. "No. And I'm pretty sure if you said that to his face, if you weren't dead already, he'd kill you."

"What he doesn't know can't come back to hurt me," he trilled and vanished from sight.

I opened the door to find Rick standing there with his hat in hand. "Sorry to interrupt on the weekend."

"Come on in. We've still got plenty of food if

you're hungry and I'm brewing a fresh pot of coffee. It's even one of Ginny's special roasts."

"Thanks for the offer, but I'm on duty. I was hoping to speak with Mrs. Henley."

"She's through there in the dining room. Is everything okay?" I thought Chloe had given her statement to the authorities upon her rescue.

"Just a few loose ends to tie up. Nothing to worry about, but there are some details her husband may not be ready to hear."

My stomach did a flip before watching him pass through the kitchen out of sight. I picked up on the sound of his voice as he entered the dining room and asked to speak with Chloe for a moment.

"Whatever you need to ask her, you can say in front of the rest of us. We don't have secrets," Max protested.

"It's fine, Max. Really. Why don't you go see if Darcy needs any help in the kitchen?"

After a brief moment of silence, I heard a chair move, and footsteps sounded in my direction. I busied myself with the coffee pot, hoping he didn't think I'd been eavesdropping. Max walked in and glanced over his shoulder just as I caught Rick moving further into the house, likely to speak with Chloe in private.

"You shouldn't worry. Rick's just wrapping up the investigation. I'm sure he only wants to make sure that they've got everything they need to make an iron clad case," I explained, hoping to reassure the man.

"I know. I get the feeling something else happened while she was being held captive and she's not ready to tell me about it."

"I'm sorry. That's got to be so frustrating."

"When she's ready, I'll be waiting." He leaned his forearms on the edge of the counter by the sink, staring at the decorative backsplash. "My life hasn't always been the neatest thing. If you can't tell, I'm kind of a mess. But Chloe always got me. She accepted the mess and never complained. And she never tried to fix me, you know?"

"I do. She loved you for you, flaws and all."

"I like to think that came down to our parents raising both me and Maggie right. At least in how they taught us to treat the people we love."

"Well, I'd say they did a wonderful job. Everyone struggles, even if it's not obvious to the people around them. And the demons you've had to face don't make you a bad person."

He let out a slow breath. "You and Maggie have been together a while. Longer than a lot of her past relationships. You make her feel safe. I could see that even in just the few days I've been here. That's all I've wanted for my sister."

"Uh ... thanks for the vote of confidence." He stared at me so intently I couldn't help but shift my weight under the intensity of his gaze. "So, why do I get the feeling I'm about to get the protective brother speech?"

His hands kneaded together in front of him. "I've never actually had to give the speech before."

"Uh oh."

"There's never been anyone really worth giving it to." He spun so his back now rested against the counter's edge. "You love my sister. That's obvious. And she's head over heels in love with you. But she's been burned once before with ... taking things to the next level."

"I know she was engaged once, and it didn't work out. They never exchanged vows."

"Everyone was glad for that, believe me. But this feels different."

"You think she's going to propose?" I rasped.

"After last time, I don't think she wants to be the one to do the asking."

I let his words sink in for a long moment, the coffee pot announcing it had finished brewing in the background. "I mean ... before moving here I hadn't ever really pictured myself getting married. Not that it wasn't a possibility mind you, just no one back in England really felt right."

"She feels right?" he filled in.

"She does. But there are things that make it complicated." The fear that she'd think me proposing was somehow some sort of ploy for residency status flashed through my mind.

"So, uncomplicate it. I just wanted you to know that, and not that you need it, but you've got my blessing when the time comes."

"You're awful confident that it will come soon," I noted.

"I may have been gypped on the family magic front, but I've got a sense about this sort of thing. You two make each other happy and I can't see a reason you shouldn't at least be able to pop the question. Stay engaged as long as you want, but don't let my sister get away. Not when you two fit together like two puzzle pieces."

I stood there speechless as he reached around me and picked up the now-full coffee pot, disappearing into the dining room to refill cups as if nothing had just happened. My head spun as his words chased themselves around my mind. Saying

Maggie and I are a perfect fit. Giving me his blessing. I had a sense that Maggie might have been thinking of taking our relationship to the next level over the summer, but nothing had come of it. I let out a small hiccup of giddy laughter as the idea truly sunk in. I could do this. I could propose to the woman who'd captured my heart from the very first moment we met.

"Everything okay out there?" Maggie stuck her head through the opening between the kitchen and dining room.

"Everything's grand," I answered, rushing forward to pull her into an embrace. "I'm just marveling at the fact that I'm lucky to have you in my life. And thinking that it had to be more than just chance that I ended up here on holiday all those months ago."

"Feeling a little sentimental all of a sudden, are we?"

"Max just reminded me of how much this place means to me. It's important to have roots. You'd think as a hedge witch that would be obvious to me. But sometimes, I suppose I just take for granted that I've been able to grow here both as a witch and a person."

"Remind me not to leave you alone with my

brother for prolonged periods of time. He makes everyone sentimental. Come on, let's get back in there before he steals all the coffee."

I chuckled as we rejoined our company at the dining room table. Chloe had returned and Rick hesitated at the far end of the room, eyeing the spread. "Oh, just sit down already, Rick. You've done your job," Tania invited, waving him over.

"Everyone is family here," I declared as he joined us, grabbing one of the last waffles on the serving dish.

As I surveyed the people around the table, I realized just how true that statement was going to be some day. In that moment I resolved that before the year was out, I was going to make Maggie Henley my fiancée.

## A QUICK AUTHOR'S NOTE

I'LL BE HONEST, when I started planning this book, it was supposed to be rather light-hearted. Yes, there was going to be drama and suspense, but it was supposed to be about family.

Yeah, that kind of went off the rails quickly! I

honestly am not sure why my brain led me down the path of human trafficking but once it was there, it felt right. It still gave us a chance to see Maggie and her family and get to know a little more about their history and dynamic. I still remember writing the very end of chapter two and going, yeah Max would absolutely have a pet name for Maggie that she *hates*. And I did quite enjoy seeing them both struggle to be in each other's lives and how by the end, they were in a much better place.

And of course, Max's blessing at the end is a huge piece of where Darcy's story is going next. In fact, it fully informs much of the plot of the next book.

*Turn the page to ake a peek at what's coming for Darcy in High Court...*

<u>HIGH COURT</u>

**Will the real Darcy Ingram please stand up?**

Change is on Darcy's mind as summer turns to autumn in Brookhaven once more. Firmly a part of the Brookhaven community, Darcy longs to make a more permanent change. And with her relationship with Maggie headed full-steam ahead towards longevity, she's ready to take the next step and obtain her Green card.

What should have been a simple interview quickly spirals out of control as the officer accuses Darcy of thing she's never done—things she can't have done. And the more she protests, the more vehemently he presses her. The threat of being detained spurs Darcy to get to the bottom of what must be a mistaken identity.

But when the officer winds up dead in his office, Darcy has more reason to get to the bottom things. Clearing her own name is only the beginning. She'll have to rely on her ever-growing magic to root out the culprit and the real intended target. Because for once, she's not the only Darcy Ingram in the crosshairs.

*Scan the QR code to get High Court*

# ABOUT THE AUTHOR

S.E. Biglow is the pen name of *USA Today* bestselling author Sarah Biglow. She lives in Massachusetts with her husband and son. She is a licensed attorney and spends her days combatting employment discrimination as an Investigator with the Mass-achusetts Commission Against Discrimination.

You can find an up-to-date list of all my books here